A Summer Night In Norway

by

Martin Aspelund

For Leonine

1

Boats slithered gently through the Oslofjord on a warm evening at the dawn of summer. Rickard walked along the local harbor as usual, enjoying all the strange people passing by. The screams and laughter of children afforded him great joy; it reminded him of happy, youthful memories. The summertime in Drøbak is very special, and many Norwegians visit during the warmer months. It's a charming little village in the gracious fjord leading into Norway's capital. Around fifteen thousand people live in and around the town, and nearly everyone knows each other. There is a shortage of secrets in small towns like these and a great deal of gossip-hungry inhabitants who desire to know what's happening in every household. Rickard was one amongst this little tribe, lying on the outskirts of Oslo.

Yet, he did not live as the townsfolk did; his bed was underneath the open sky. That was, for most of the year anyway. He always stayed outside as long as he could. For the past eight years, he had lived in Drøbak by sleeping on a park bench from late April till late October. In the remaining months of the year, a kind-hearted woman named Martha had let him sleep in her annex. His bench, which he had baptized Abraham Lincoln, was placed near the local supermarket in the city center. On both sides, the old wooden bench was surrounded by heavy bushes, with birch trees reaching out from behind. This made his *bed* look rather sequestered, which was further aided by a green tarp Rickard would wrap around it during the daytime. He found it agreeable to be slightly out of sight while still remaining close to people.

Rickard's sleeping area was well organized. In the morning, he would wrap up Abraham with all his sleeping gear placed inside. It contained a pillow and a sleeping bag, both of which he had owned for a long time. That people leave park benches wrapped up alone was something he had been delighted to discover years ago. However, people are curious about such an unusual phenomenon. People would often glance at the strange arrangement, but were simply too embarrassed, or maybe polite, to cause any trouble. Behind the bench, in the vegetative thickness, he kept an old suitcase with other necessities. The luggage contained hygiene products, his groceries, two full outfits he mixed and matched throughout the week, and an old book. This was also wrapped in a green tarp, and he had only experienced theft once: a six-pack of beer, which wasn't bad considering how long he had been staying there. At around six p.m. every day, he would return to Abe and begin settling for the night. He would undo the tarp, place it in his suitcase, then sit on the bench and observe the world as it passed before him.

To survive, Rickard collected bottles from the trash bins around town. The bottles could be recycled at the local supermarket for a small amount, between one and two kroner per bottle. There was plenty to find, especially after the weekends. The park and the city square were littered with people on the weekend, with a significant surge in visitors during the warmer months. This created a bottle haven for Rickard, which he rapidly realized after arriving in the small town. By spending about four to five hours collecting bottles on Mondays, he usually turned over one to two thousand kroner, which he spread over the week. He survived well in that region of *wealth* if one can venture to call it that. However, some days, particularly as the seasons turned colder, there wouldn't be much to collect, causing prolonged periods of meagerness. In case of disaster, Rickard had collected a small emergency fund, which he had placed in the lining of his suitcase, inside a little black bag; tucked away were 3,000 kroner he had been able to gather over a few years.

The habit of generating money by collecting bottles he had picked up after arriving in Norway. At first, he found the act of rummaging through trash bins awfully uncomfortable. It was a rather dirty undertaking, literally speaking, but worst of all were the nasty glances thrown at him. Yet with time, as with all else, his shame dwindled and disappeared. 'I'm not hurting a soul, and I'm simply expediting the recycling of the metals and plastics,' he concluded, although it took time to arrive there.

As he was closing in on his ninth year in Drøbak, he had observed and thought for a while. The mind travels to strange places with enough time, particularly in social isolation. Living beneath the open sky provides little status, and it turns out that people's compassion, at the very least outside of family, is directed sideways or upwards in the status hierarchy. And where compassion is lacking, other insidious feelings follow. Rickard practically spent all his time alone. When he sat on his bench, no one approached him; all he received were crude comments, distasteful glances, and the odd hollow smile. What a sad and irresponsible soul, their eyes would scream. Those experiences, day in and day out, are enough to turn any man against the world. For Rickard, it caused a love of mankind and nature. And he grew disappointed with individuals, so his focus didn't linger there.

Apart from Martha, who took pity on the old man when he arrived in Drøbak, there was only one boy he had some affection for. August Linberg was his name. He had introduced himself to Rickard years ago: the young boy was heading into a grocery store when he saw Rickard. He strolled straight over to the old man sitting on his usual bench and asked him whether he needed anything. The kindness in his eyes was almost matched by his handsome features. Rickard was moved by the gesture but declined the offer. From thereon, their relationship developed slowly as August continually struck up conversations whenever he saw him.

The routine evening walk, which Rickard found himself on that day, always started by the local harbor. He was fond of boats and the water, so he spent considerable time there, either sitting down or strolling back and forth, admiring veteran boats and the newly arriving ones. He rejoiced in the absurdity of how these frail structures fought and prevailed against the overwhelming forces of nature herself.

After the harbor, he had moved into a nearby park bordering the water. Shortly after entering, the path diverged, and he would be forced to choose between continuing deeper into the park or heading to the city's graveyard and church. Rickard preferred the dead to the living, so that choice was easy. He was always struck by the fact that all those erect stones, on that large patch of ovulated grass, represented men and women who had led lives like his; a sea of lifetimes lay before him.

'I bet each of them thought they'd live forever,' he had told August once. We all end up there – in the ground – but it's exceptionally difficult to fathom. The realization is painful, and mundane distraction jumps in to help us repress this unpleasant fact. Inevitably, however, the music stops, and the illusion drops. Much like your dead relatives, you will also end up resting in the ground. But what happens when you pass the threshold? Is there somewhere? God only knows. The trick, Rickard had found, was to turn the impossible realization of death into something positive; namely, that it imbues the present with its true significance.

As he moved slowly past the gravestones of all those strangers, he spotted a familiar person tending to a grave. Rickard opened the gate and strolled over to a frail woman in a neat red summer dress with flower-petaled patterns.

'Hello Martha, how's Bjørn today?'

'Same old, same old. These flowers, however, could use some more water. That pesky sun is relentless, really!' she exclaimed, shaking her fist upward.

'In any case, don't you want to come stay at my place a little earlier this year, dear? The nights are getting colder and colder…' she continued, looking meekly at the old fellow.

'No, thank you. You know very well I prefer it outside as long as I can bear it. These months are the best times of year, too,' he replied.

She agreed these were good months indeed, and they stood there looking at the beautifully tended grave for a while.

'Oh, look at the time. I better be off; I'm meeting a few friends in town for dinner,' she said, patting his back. 'I'm already looking forward to November, and do stop by for tea at any time!'

What a special person she is, he thought, as the warm sensation of gratitude filled him.

'I'll do that,' he replied and waved her onwards.

The stroll continued past the graveyard, and at the far end of the plot, the local Protestant church was placed. It was a small, unimpressive building painted light blue, with a black clock fixed above the main entrance. As he passed the church, he glanced up, where the clock showed five to six. Rickard had been inside there several times and even prayed, but he didn't consider himself a religious man. If we are honest, who hasn't prayed once or twice despite doubting the existence of God? He noted the time as he passed, thinking he would get back to Lincoln a little later than usual.

On the way home, he walked past a few people enjoying the weakened strength of the evening sun. Not one of them, however, met Rickard's inviting gaze. It didn't surprise him. He was used to it, but it still tinged his heart a little. As no one spoke to him, he had taken up the habit of talking to himself while walking about town. This didn't help with growing his social circle or with the menacing looks, but Rickard didn't care. He didn't care much about anything. He was a free man, and nothing bothered or excited the old man anymore.

He had started to grow rather apathetic to life, but he still managed to find pleasure in a few things: being in Martha's company was one, beer was another, and the last was the conversations shared with August. Normally, the young man would stop by Abraham and Rickard's once or twice a week. They would talk about what was going on in August's life, trivial things, and sometimes they would stumble onto deep and important matters. In all honesty, the topics of conversation mattered little to the old man; he enjoyed sharing a dialog with a compassionate fellow.

'Good to see you again, Abe!' he exclaimed as he approached his park bench.

'Today's walk was lovely, I'll tell you. The weather smiled, and the birds sang their lovely tunes. I even ran into Martha on the way back. I'll have to go by her place sometime this week, if I can find the time,' he concluded as he began unwrapping his bed for the evening.

He placed the green tarp in his suitcase and fished two cans of beer out. He took a seat on the bench, with his sleeping bag and pillow sitting on the far end of his right. He had given some thought to quitting drinking. It was both expensive and a nasty killer, devouring both brain cells and the liver. It will also wreck your life if you give it a proper chance, but that was less of a concern for the old man, given there wasn't much of a social life to destroy. It's funny, really, how this horrendous drug is ubiquitous in society – but, then again, if one didn't have the freedom to get drunk, what kind of sterile life would that be? Moreover, there is a wonderfully creative and social aspect to it! Until Rickard was thirty-four, he didn't touch alcohol. He saw how it made his friends act like idiots, and he didn't want any part of it.

Working hard and spending time with family took precedence in his life, making it easy to avoid the bottle. However, when he first got a taste for it, there was no turning back, no putting it down and returning to his peaceful existence. The blissful feeling of forgetting oneself, which everyone feels to a degree, was too valuable to give up. Rickard reminisced about this as he opened the first bottle of beer.

People streamed in and out of the grocery store before the old man, and it was nearing closing time. He didn't own a watch, but he had gotten quite good at judging the time by the weather. The reference point he got by the church every evening didn't hurt either. He figured it was close to eight p.m. by now, which was the closing time of the local supermarket. All of the various faces that walked fifty paces before him, he had seen a thousand times before. He didn't know their actual names, but he had awarded them names nonetheless, even stories when he had the energy. Letting one's imagination run in this manner was a thrilling and humorous endeavor, something Rickard had discovered as a young boy.

2

The evening spilled into night, and everything was quiet as Rickard put his head to the pillow. He lay on his right side, overlooking the store entrance and part of the city square in the distance. From there, he was able to make out part of the fountain in the middle of the square, as well as two park benches facing the middle. It was a small square of cobblestone, with well-maintained trees spaced around the edges in two-meter increments. During the late-summer months, the square was always bustling with little children running around, often with ice cream in hand. As the evenings neared, the children were displaced by teenagers who would hang out, drink beers, fall in love, and enjoy the vicissitudes of adolescent life. That evening, however, there was not a soul. There was utter silence; all that could be heard was a tinge of music in the distance; it might have been Oasis playing, but it was difficult to tell. Rickard enjoyed a dimly noticeable buzz, as he had just finished his second beer before lying down.

The old man was content, and life felt bearable. 'I don't know about you, Abe, but things could be a lot worse,' he mumbled. He often reflected on how he had ended up here, in the charming little town of Drøbak, sleeping on the streets. He had first learned of the place when he returned to Norway, but had never visited before arriving here eight years ago. By now, he had grown fond of the place. It had a peculiar charm. A little Nordic paradise placed in the mouth of the Oslofjord. While his gaze was fixed upon the firmament, the thought of death entered his mind. He wondered whether he would die here. He thought it wouldn't be bad to have this as your final resting place. What caused him concern was the act of dying, not being dead. He was scared of pain; there didn't seem to be anything more painful than dying, he had understood, after being present at that final leap for several loved ones. 'The agonizing cry of despair at the end. It never fails. It is always there, and it's visceral,' he would tell anyone willing to listen to him ramble on about death. That wasn't a whole lot; death isn't a popular topic of conversation—although, maybe it ought to be.

Two men walked along the edges of the square, disagreeing over some matter, evident by their tones of voice. Rickard was awoken and could tell both men were rather displeased by the steadily rising volume of their voices. He turned his tired body to face the square to get a better look at the situation. They had awakened him from his slumber, which was no easy task, as he slept deeply like a hibernating beast. He saw two teenagers having a heated exchange with beers in hand. 'I wonder if they have any to spare,' he thought, as one of the fellows pushed the other. 'Oh well, they better calm down before somebody's feelings get hurt.' He made out some of their conversation now, as their voices continued to rise.

'Who the fuck do you think you are, meddling in my business? Leave me and my relationship the hell alone.'

'It's not much of a relationship, that. Who would want to be in a relationship with a monster like you?'

'Josephine, apparently,' he laughed maliciously.

'Leave her alone; she doesn't know what she wants.'

'She did know she wanted me more than you. That much I know.'

It became quiet for a while, and only the self-righteous satisfaction of the man who had hurled the last comment was felt.

'Perhaps, but violating her is unacceptable either way,' a hurt voice eventually retorted.

'Shut your mouth; you really have no idea what you're talking about,' he shouted as he reached his hand out and poured the rest of his beer over the other man's head.

He stood still for a second with his soaking wet head hanging down, then he turned his body slightly and let a punch fly, aimed straight at the man's face. It landed square, and so did the poor fellow's body on the cobblestoned ground. A ghastly noise escaped at impact. The boy's arms were spread out now. He lay still, gazing up at the wondrous night sky. The man fell to his knees and slapped his face gently.

'Hey! Hey! Hello, Mathias!' he said with a trembling voice.

No response. Down on his knees, he continued trying to make contact, but to no avail. Realizing that he couldn't wake him, he looked up toward the heavens and clenched his face in utter despair.

'Dear Lord, what have I done…'

As he muttered those words, a hand touched the young man's shoulder and he jumped up in terror.

'I saw what happened. Is he gone?' Rickard queried.

The young man's eyes were as wild as a raging river, and his whole body shook sporadically.

'Take a few deep breaths. You will be all right; it was an accident,' he continued.

He felt sorry for August at that moment. Naturally, he hadn't meant for this to happen, yet the prospects of his life had just turned dim. Unintentional actions can make all the difference, went through Rickard's mind, as he placed a paternal hand on the desolate boy's shoulder. Sobbing cries left August, but he was glad that the old man was there.

They stood there for a while with Rickard's arm resting on August, both waiting for the world to catch up with all its terrible consequences. Before it had the chance, however, showers of rain began falling upon them.

'We need to move him,' Rickard said resolutely. 'Here, we'll bring him up like this,' he continued and acted it out awkwardly.

'Just like we're carrying an obliterated friend.'

The young man didn't say a word but helped Rickard bring the body up and placed its arms around their necks.

'Here, this way! We'll head toward the park; it shouldn't take more than a few minutes,' he said as they began moving back toward Abraham. When they made it to his bed, Rickard left August alone for a second as he went rummaging behind the bushes. He came out with a long piece of rope, which he normally used to fasten the tarp to the bench during the day.

'We will need this,' he stated with a forced smile.

August didn't seem to register what was happening exactly, but maybe it was better, thought Rickard. They made their way over to the park, which hugged the waterline. There was a small stretch in the park where one could walk off the path onto rugged grass terrain. After walking a small incline, you would be standing on a cliff that stood a few meters above the water. It was about the only place where the water grew deep close to the shoreline. Apart from the odd teenager cliff jumping, no one ventured there. As they neared the spot, it dawned on August what was happening and where they were going.

'I… I can't...' he stuttered, then he released Mathias's weight and stepped to the side. 'I can't do this. What the hell are we doing?'

Rickard looked him dead in his terrified eyes. 'Unless you want to rot away in a cell for the better part of your life, you need to do this.'

He didn't enjoy speaking harshly to August, but it was necessary. It was paramount that he understood the gravity of the situation. There was a sliver of hope that they could dispose of the body successfully. The rain would hopefully wash away the blood from the dragging of the body; however, they also needed to keep the body from rising to the surface upon hitting the water. There was a little campfire close by where he had planned to throw the unfortunate man out, where a few concrete blocks were placed around for people to sit on. They would be useful, but before he could give any more thought to that, he needed help to move the body the rest of the way.

'Come now, boy, the rest of your life depends on this. You have committed an unforgivable sin; this won't make it worse.' Rickard nearly screamed at the young man, who was fighting to keep his sanity.

My life is over kept ringing through August's mind. His internal voice screamed these words repeatedly, and the only response he could muster was shaking his head resolutely while gripping his temples.

'What an utter fool I am,' he mumbled with clenched teeth.

He eventually let go of his head and looked up. Before him stood a drenched old man in ragged and bloody clothes, with his dead best friend hanging onto him. He wondered for a second whether he was having a nightmare.

'Okay, let's continue before anyone sees us,' he said quickly, as he helped support the other half of the limp body.

They continued moving in tandem toward the cliff, which August had realized was where Rickard had planned to dispose of the body. When they finally reached the edge of the little cliff, some relief befell both men. Thankfully, they hadn't run into anyone on the way; the rain had probably helped keep the nightwalkers at bay that night.

'Now, we need something heavy to tie to his body. Some fifty meters that way, there are some concrete blocks used as seating for a campfire. One of those should do the trick; go and grab one for us,' he commanded August, who nodded, then ran toward the fireplace.

It only took a moment to get there, and sure enough, eight concrete blocks were placed in a circle around a fireplace. August grabbed the closest one. He picked it up rather easily and figured it couldn't weigh over fifteen kilos. He ran back, feeling disconcerted about the block's usefulness. When he arrived, he found that Rickard had tied a knot around Mathias's legs. He placed the concrete block next to the body, and Rickard threaded the rope through one of the holes in the middle of the block.

'I was a seafarer in my younger days, you see,' he said humorously as he finished the knot. 'Now grab his body, I'll carry this rock, then we'll throw them off at the count of three, alright?' he continued.

'Wait. How can you possibly know this will be enough to...'

'Trust me, alright? One. Two. Three!'

There was a loud splash that reverberated throughout the fjord, yet the night's silence quickly enveloped it. All that remained was the continually diminishing sound of small waves finishing their journey on the cliff wall where the two fatigued men stood.

3

August's life went from mildly boring to excruciatingly interesting at the turn of a fortnight. Murdering Mathias had not felt bad in the moment, exactly, although it had not been his intention; all he wanted to do was talk some sense into his old friend, as he had behaved reprehensibly. That evening had been one surprise after the other; as he stood before his bleeding body, August's body was frozen still beyond belief. He couldn't move an inch as shock held him still. Only yet another shock could drag him out of it, namely, someone's hand on his shoulder. *I've been caught, that's it* ran through his mind as he turned his head.

As fate would have it, it wasn't a normal citizen of Drøbak, but the homeless man living right outside that damned grocery nearby. He was a man August had grown fond of, as he had gotten to know him little by little over the last few years. He considered him wise and kind, despite his dilapidated facade.

At first, he figured the old man would hand him and the whole catastrophe over to the police, as he must have been the last person who wanted any trouble.

Thankfully, he was mistaken, as not only did he not give him up, but he had also helped him dispose of the body. August hadn't considered what to do, but Rickard's equanimity and resourcefulness helped solve the horrible riddle. Powers beyond him were also kind to provide a shower of rain to wash away the traces of his sins; he felt as if the world was conspiring to help him.

When he arrived home that night, drenched in water and a few blood stains, he didn't feel at home in his body. It was as if someone had taken possession of him, and he stood to the side, observing what was happening. His parents were fast asleep, thankfully, and he grabbed a trash bag from the kitchen and went straight to his room. He threw all of his clothes in the bag, closed it, and then placed it underneath the bed. He lay down, naked with spread legs, as his hands came up and began gripping his head and wet hair. 'What the fuck,' he kept muttering repeatedly.

Slowly, it dawned on him what happened. What he had done. Until that moment, it was as if he had been walking in an unintelligible fog. All at once, a stream of wonderful memories he had shared with Mathias flooded his mind, and he began sobbing uncontrollably.

Unlike Promethius who had given the spark of light, he had stolen the life spark from one of the most important people in his life; how could one possibly live with oneself after that?

He felt the terrible grief of losing one's best friend in the marrow of his bones, and the pain he had caused for Mathias's loving family was perhaps even worse. He lay there crying for hours, naked and alone in utter hysteria, as his mind edged closer to insanity; he felt less fixed in his being, as if his grip on reality was loosening, which caused tremendous alarm in the young man. It made him feel uneasy, and creeping thoughts of having to be admitted to an asylum were impossible to fend off. He looked up at the spinning ceiling fan, wondering, 'If I ever regain my normalcy, where do I go from here?'

The next morning, he was utterly sleep-deprived, but somehow his mental faculties were sharp.

'You look like a mess, August. And you weren't home when we went to sleep yesterday. When did you get back?' his mother asked, rather concerned, as he stepped into the kitchen.

'I didn't sleep too well, must've been the alcohol. Mathias and I had a few beers yesterday evening, and I lost track of time, but it was nice to catch up,' he said, walking toward the fridge to search for some cheese and jam.

'Ah, did you see Mathias yesterday?' she said with a smile. 'I'm so happy to see the two of you spending time together again.'

August gave a slight nod.

'You should get to bed early tonight, so you'll be ready for the week to come sweetheart,' she continued, placing a cup of steaming coffee before him.

'I'm off for a run; remember to get some sunlight, and don't sit before that wretched computer all day. Love you,' she said, kissing his cheek, and then she disappeared out the door. He sat there alone, and the weight on his shoulders felt unbearable, crushing his weakened spirit further. *If only she knew,* he thought, attempting to hold back his tears.

He sipped the coffee, then took two slices of bread from a cutting board placed on the table. A slice of cheese with butter and one with jam were consumed slowly. His appetite was lacking, but he figured he needed to force some energy into himself. As he gnawed at the bread, August replayed the events of yesterday evening. It felt surreal. However, before stepping downstairs, he had checked whether there was a bag of clothes underneath his bed. Just in case he had suffered from some awful nightmare, but sure enough, there it was, smelling of humidity and blood.

He glanced at the time; it was 9:45 AM now. His father, he figured, was out playing his traditional golf round with friends. He felt glad he didn't need to face him now. He concentrated once again on what had happened, trying to rack his head for any clues he might have left behind. Maybe a piece of clothing had been ripped? Did anyone spot them? Any distressful thought that emerged, he considered.

In the end, he couldn't think of anything but two problems: the first was his slightly swollen red knuckles, the other being Rickard. The first issue he didn't think would be a major problem. It didn't look bad at all, and his mother hadn't even noticed, and she was an observant lady. He grabbed a bag of frozen peas from the freezer and placed it on his aching fist. It was funny; he hadn't even noticed any pain there nor thought about it at all before those thoughts started flooding his mind.

The second problem, however, was a lot more significant, and he had no idea what to do about it. In a sense, he had also been the solution to the biggest problem there was. But that was in the past now, and he didn't know what Rickard would do; he didn't really know him at all. So why had he helped him? That aside, as he had helped hide the body, there was little chance he would turn August in, he concluded after a bit of dreadful reflection. Yet, not knowing who he really was caused unrest in the young man. He wondered if there was a way he could place the blame on him, coming out of it unscathed himself, yet it seemed utterly evil and unlikely. Rickard had clarified the path forward for August yesterday; his life could take two very different paths—it was all up to him.

A part of him longed to do the right thing, to turn himself in and face the consequences of his actions. Simultaneously, the thought of losing the greater part of his life and his freedom gripped him. 'Perhaps the body wouldn't be found and he would simply be deemed missing, presumed to have run away somewhere,' was the hope he held dear to his heart. He attempted to weigh his possible decisions carefully. If he turned himself in, all his loved ones would turn away from him for the rest of his life, with good reason. *That can't happen; I'd rather die*. No, he would deny all involvement in the murder no matter what. And staying well away from Rickard was another good idea, he thought, and so with that, he felt minimally at peace, having put up some reasonable rules for how to proceed.

It was time to get his mind somewhere different and let it rest. He couldn't bear thinking about it anymore, yet he was pleasantly surprised that he managed to think somewhat coherently about the situation, despite murdering someone he cared dearly about only hours ago. He went upstairs to play on his computer, but as he entered the room a moist bag could be seen sticking out from under his bed. *Best get rid of that first*, he thought.

4

The next morning, Rickard went to get another rope. He wrapped up his bed, as usual, and made for his morning spot. There was a place tucked away inside a little forest nearby, where Rickard enjoyed spending his mornings. It took about twenty minutes to walk there when he felt energetic. This time, however, he took over half an hour. On the way, he pondered yesterday's happenings. What had compelled him to help that young man? He searched and asked, but could find no satisfactory answer. Yet, his mind wasn't uneasy exactly. He felt content about helping the young man, as he had a good heart. The horrid circumstances didn't change that.

A thick forest made up of pine trees and oaks was scattered around an undulating area two kilometers north-west of the city center. There were two ponds in the forest, one small and the other a little larger. By the smallest pond, called Jungsdammen, there was a large stone, resting partly above and partly below the surface of the quiet water. On this rock, Rickard had found a magnificent stillness. He had discovered this precious spot, overlooking the pond and surrounding forest, about three years back. Ever since then, he returned there religiously during the months he slept outside. It brought him a great deal of comfort and nostalgia, as it reminded him of a pond he had visited many times as a child living in England.

He met a few people in the forest: an older couple walking together, and the rest were people out for their morning dog walks. At a certain point, he went off the walking path and threaded through some rough terrain before the trees opened up and revealed a small body of water. Rickard slowly placed himself on the stone and took a few deep breaths. He wondered what was going to happen from here as he surveyed the water sprawling with life.

As August had a good heart, he was unsure whether the boy could keep the events concealed. 'If he knows what's good for him, he will stay quiet, but I suspect a reminder wouldn't hurt,' he thought. Next time they see each other, he would remind him of what hung in the balance. Rickard was also curious to understand what could have caused him to punch that poor fellow. It seemed out of character, as August seemed like a mild-tempered person. He made a mental note to ask that too.

Rickard's hands were placed slightly behind him, carrying the weight of his upper body, while his head hung slightly back. His eyes were closed, and he took delight in feeling the sun resting on his eyelids. He sat still and listened; a world was unfolding around him. He heard the sweetness of birds singing, insects scavenging, and fish jumping. Everything was moving and changing around him, as everything does in this world. *We are all simple visitors, passing by for a while* lingered in his mind.

Eventually, he opened his eyes again and felt it was time to read a few passages. He fished an old book out of his left-hand blazer pocket. It was Arthur Waley's translation of the Tao Te Ching. He had picked it up from a used bookshop in London about three decades back. Rickard found a rejuvenating spring of wisdom in the poetic writings of Lao-Tzu. He opened the book at random and began reading. After a while, he put the book down sat there, observing once more. He alternated between the two for some time before eventually getting up. He didn't want to stay there too long. He was worried about growing tired of the special place he had found, so he only afforded himself a little peace at this secluded spot. Another reason was the frightening compulsion to never want to leave the forest. He reminded himself he had a little longer still.

He made his way out of the forest and toward the town. As he strolled back, he remembered that Martha had invited him over for tea. 'That'll please her,' he murmured and decided to see whether she was home. Martha's house was only about two hundred and fifty meters from the city square. There was a street with a little incline, called Damveien, that led up toward her plot. A hundred meters up the road, you would turn onto a side street that led to her house. It was a beautiful, narrow street, with little overhanging trees and multi-colored fences demarcating the various houses. Her house was the fifth in the row, on the right-hand side, when you turned into the street. It was a charming wooden house, which is the common material used for housing in Norway, painted dark yellow with white window frames. It was a two-story house, but she didn't use the second floor much, as climbing the flight of stairs at her age was an extreme sport. Only when her kids visited would those rooms be used. She had a little patio that she adored, where she would often sit, drinking tea alone or with friends, or knitting something for her grandchildren. Her husband had built the patio, she told

Rickard, years ago. There was also a small garden in front of the house, with two flowerbeds on either side of the wooden gateway. A white fence was placed neatly around the plot, and the path from her fenced gateway, leading to her patio and front door, was paved with red stone bricks.

Rickard walked slowly up the narrow side street, enjoying the scenery immensely. The gardens were scattered with blossoming apple trees, flowering bushes, and grass greener than first-year police officers. There was no one around now, but on weekends, these gardens would be filled with children dancing and joyful adults sharing wonderful memories.

He reached Martha's white fence and saw her sitting by herself, knitting something or other, on her patio with a thin smile. He smiled to himself as he stood there observing the merry old woman, blissfully unaware of the world around her. As he went to open the gateway, she realized he was arriving and shouted at him with a beaming smile, 'Rickard! What a wonderful surprise! I'll put on the kettle. Take a seat here, dear; I'll be right back!'

She stormed out of her chair and into the kitchen. This produced a jovial mood in the old man, and he made his way up to the patio, sitting down by her little wooden table. A few moments later, she came strolling out with an apron and a delighted look on her face. 'The tea should be ready in a few minutes. Can I offer you anything else?' she asked as she placed a round metal box on the table with a mixture of crackers and sweets.

'That'll do just fine, Martha. Thank you. Sit down, sit down now!' he replied, motioning at her chair.

'How is it going, dear?'

'Just fine, just fine. I was up by the forest earlier; there were plenty of raspberries waiting to be picked! The weather is also so agreeable these days, aside from last night's downfall. What's not to love?'

'We should be thankful for a little rain, too. And yes! That's a wonderful idea! I haven't made jam in ages. I'll take my daughter this weekend if she has the time.'

'And how about you?' he followed up quickly.

'Same old here, I'm doing well. Spending time with friends, children, and grandchildren raises the spirits! But I must admit, I long for the days when Bjørn waltzed around the kitchen and living room, singing his favorite tunes. I look forward to seeing him again.'

'On the other side?'

'Mhm.' She nodded softly.

'Well, I'm happy to have you here on our side for now, and I believe I'm speaking on behalf of all of us.'

'So am I,' she said, before heading back into the kitchen to fetch the tea. As she was inside, Rickard got to thinking about mortality once more. In the latter part of his life, it happened often that his train of thought swerved onto the lane of death. It was something he had considered a great deal, and he felt at ease with the idea of vanishing by now. Before he was born, he was dead, in a sense, and he didn't have any ill feelings about that, so why should the time after life be any different? He felt one should rejoice in death! It seems to be the precondition for the significance of the present moment. Imagine being immortal: all things would lose significance, and nothing would be special, as everything would lack that bittersweet tinge of death. Lost in these thoughts, Rickard looked meekly across her lawn. Moments later, he was pulled out of his introversion with Martha swinging out the door. She held a steaming teapot and two cups, which she placed before him. A green cup with white petals was shoved before Rickard, which she subsequently filled with steaming liquid. She repeated the process for herself, although she had opted for a cup with the words *World's Best Grandma* plastered across it.

'Now, what does a woman need to do to entice a man to stay in her annex all year round?' she threw out humorously as she sat down.

Rickard smiled widely while he crossed his arms. He shook his head gently and said, 'You won't stop, will you? You are about the sweetest person I've met, Martha. I am so grateful to you for letting me stay here for a few months of the year. That is more than enough, and to tell you the truth, I find an immense sense of harmony in sleeping under the stars. That's the reason I do it, and you know as well as I that I don't have to.'

'I simply don't get it. What is so harmonious about sleeping outside without shelter, warmth, and any money to your name, Rickard?'

'One reason I enjoy it, this free life, is that I adore the childlike nature of it all. It's a little like stepping outside our artificial, self-imposed troubles. Out of time. You're forced to live in harmony with the most relentless woman there is: Nature. It is like taking up the role of the Original Man; Adam is once more your brother, and the animals too. It is a stepping into a timelessness that's always lurking behind our daily trivialities and catastrophes. Martha, that's where life is; that's where it always was.'

'All of that sounds poetic and great, but I'd much rather sleep in the warmth of my blankets, in my soft bed and heated house. I come out on my patio or take a walk to interact with this woman you speak of.'

'I perfectly understand; hell, I was just like you for over half my life. To want a comfortable life is only natural, but I prefer a fullness of life and spirit these days.'

'But what do you mean you feel like a child exactly? How's that a good thing? You're quite the old man, if you hadn't noticed!'

'Haha, yes, so my wretched body keeps reminding me. You know as well as I do that children are superior to adults. I mean that the life of the homeless is filled with the terrifying wonder of the world. It's a pure life like nothing else; the only parallel to be drawn is the life of the child. Tell me, do you remember being a young girl, Martha?'

She remained quiet and thinking for a while. Then a smile grew upon her aged face as her eyes glimmered like stars.

'Yes, I do have a few memories. I had three brothers growing up, as you might recall, and my father ran the only grocery store where we lived. They were always sweet and protective of me. I particularly remember this one incident during the war, when a large care package landed on our little island off the coast. It had food, clothes, that kind of thing. As my father was in charge of the food supply, being the only grocer in our little town, he was responsible for distributing the aid. My father and brothers placed me on top of the pile, and I handed out things to all our fellow townsfolk. I felt like Cleopatra. It was a magnificent time.'

'Yes, that sounds delightful. And your brothers now?'

'All dead, unfortunately.'

'I'm sorry.'

'So am I, but that's the price we pay. Next time it'll be me,' she joked, and Rickard smiled politely.

Eventually, the conversation dried up, and they plunged into a sweet silence that only the elderly find so effortlessly.

5

Several days went by, and nothing out of the ordinary happened. The only change was that August didn't come to visit the old man anymore. Rickard understood his apprehension and refrained from passing any judgement. He was simply content with having followed his intuition, and that August still had a chance at a normal life.

However, as the days grew in number, a strange atmosphere began to spread across the little town of Drøbak. Parents began holding their children a little closer, and friends spoke furtively among themselves. Rickard saw the shift developing before him and had an inkling as to the cause; it didn't take a genius.

These fears were positively affirmed when one day he glimpsed the front page of Aftenbladet, a renowned national newspaper, sitting on a stand in front of the local supermarket:

Young man (18) missing from Drøbak
Parents, Steinar & Mari, are pleading all to come forward with information that may lead to the discovery of their beloved son

This was the text placed into one of the boxes of the front page, on top of a handsome teenager's face. A face he had seen once before. It sent pulsing surges of despair through the frail man's body. He collected his nerves and wandered back to his bench.

'How'll the boy handle this?' he asked Abraham, as he figured an investigation would be launched. August was the last person to see that boy. If others knew that, which didn't seem unlikely, it could mean trouble for the young man.

Later that evening, close to midnight, the troubled young man awakened him: 'Rickard!' he exclaimed as he stumbled towards the sleepy and untidy man. 'W-what have I done?' His voice was trembling.

He noted his abnormal demeanor, to say the least. His speech was erratic, and he worried the young fellow was edging on a psychotic break.

Rickard looked at him with meek eyes; the child was a wreck. His eyes were empty and darting wildly from side to side.

'You didn't mean for any of this to happen, August. Come now. Here, take a seat, young man,' he requested, motioning for him to sit down next to him. August obliged, collapsing next to him. His eyes were fixed on the square fifty meters ahead, where the horrific act had taken place.

'Everything feels surreal, artificial even since that evening. It feels like I'm in a video game.'

'I assure you, both this and what happened is unfortunately very real. Yet it doesn't have to get worse. With time, you'll ease into existence again, trust me.'

August mumbled something indiscernible in response, as his fingers frantically tapped his thighs.

'Did anyone know you were one of the last people to see your friend?' he continued, and August nodded affirmatively.

'Alright, has anyone attempted to talk to you about that night?'

'No, not really. Someone from the police is supposed to come by school on Monday. They want to speak to several of us…' barely escaped his thin lips, before he hopelessly exclaimed, 'Ah! It'll be a fucking disaster! To hell with it, I should just tell them what happened.'

'Okay, relax now. Take a deep breath,' Rickard replied before lapsing into thought for a moment.

'You realize what's at stake, I trust. If you tell them anything, arouse any doubt, your life, as you know it, will be done for. You will spend the best years of your life shackled and prevented from exploring this magnificent world.'

He felt apprehensive about how to phrase the situation, particularly given the state of the young man. However, he once more felt it was necessary to hand him the unsavory truth.

August ran his hands frantically through his hair, back and forth many times, as he attempted to absorb what the homeless man was telling him.

'I know. I know, it's just so damn difficult to function normally. I want to feel like myself again. I'm unable to sleep, my appetite is horrendous; to tell you the truth, it already feels like my life is over. And the thought of rotting away in a prison with every loved one abandoning me, with good reason, is utterly unbearable. I think I'm going mad,' he told Rickard, with his head covered by his hands and resting on his knees. His cheeks grew red and drenched as tears escaped his despairing being.

'It won't come to that,' replied Rickard warmly, placing his arm around him. The loving embrace felt good, and August wished he had never let go. As they sat there, the old man asked him who the boy was.

'Why do you ask?' he replied, feeling hurt and not comprehending why it mattered.

'I don't know exactly, I just felt compelled to ask. And frankly, I'd like to understand how this happened.' He paused for a moment, then continued. 'Why did you punch him, August?'

He looked down at his feet, feeling melancholic. He didn't want to tell Rickard anything but felt he would betray the man who had helped him by not telling him the truth. He continued solemnly with his eyes still fixed on the barren ground.

'His name was Mathias. It's a long story. We go… Sorry, we went far back, as far as I can recall. We met in kindergarten, became best friends, and have been ever since. There was not one person in this world I trusted more than him. Then, around the time we turned seventeen I fell madly in love with a girl. By some miracle, she reciprocated the feelings.'

He stopped for a moment and a slight smile crept onto his otherwise despondent face, as the endearing thought of her made him glad. For a moment he remembered life wasn't only horrible and devious, there was tenderness and delight too.

'I can still remember the first time we kissed, I swear, it felt as if I was levitating! Anyway, we dated for a while and at some point, she started turning cold to my touch. I didn't understand it at all. That was, until one day, by chance I was passing her house by car. I saw Mathias on foot, heading into her driveway. My heart was ripped out of my bosom, thrown to the floor and stamped to death by the two. Then and there, I lost my greatest friend and love. Afterward, I avoided Mathias like a convicted rapist, yet that turns out to be difficult when you hang out in similar crowds. I tried my best, as I couldn't stand being in the same room as him.

Then, a few weeks ago now, a friend of mine told me that Mathias had laid a hand on Josephine. Did I mention her name earlier? It doesn't matter. I didn't believe him, of course. However, later that week, I saw her at school, and sure enough, she had a black eye. Naturally, I asked her about it, and she gave some lame excuse. It didn't matter; her timid eyes revealed what'd happened. That same evening, I sent Mathias a text proposing we grab a few beers. I intended to talk about what the hell had happened, but I didn't let Mathias know. That's the story, the rest you know.'

August looked like a man on his knees before the guillotine. The old man felt a deep sympathy for the poor boy.

'There's a reason Dante placed betrayal at the greatest depth of hell,' the old man said, patting his back with a comforting hand. The young boy didn't register what Rickard was saying, but it didn't matter. There was a deep sorrow lingering in the air of the night as the moon looked woefully upon the two men.

'I'm so sorry, August.'

'So am I.'

It was quiet, and the night had placed the day in its hollow and somber hands. Both men sat on the bench, side by side, wondering how this catastrophe might develop from here.

'I'd better go home,' he muttered.

He rose slowly and gave a forced smile to the old man. 'Thank you for everything, Rickard. Whatever happens from here on is my cross to bear,' he said hesitatingly, then he turned away and walked homewards. Rickard had never felt so sorry for another man as he did now, watching that poor fellow's head hanging as he faded into the distance.

Over the next few days, the missing teenager became widespread news across the nation. Police questioned August, who told them they had enjoyed some beers that summer evening by the local harbor, but parted ways before it started pouring down. He did his best to tell them everything that happened, in accurate detail, only leaving out a few things; as we know, a great lie is mostly the truth. It also became known to the police that Mathias's girlfriend was August's ex-girlfriend, which didn't paint a pretty picture, motive-wise. Despite this, they eventually eased their focus on the young man, as everyone they spoke to only had good things to say. In the absence of any material evidence, there was nothing else for them to do. Rickard was also questioned by a gentle-mannered policeman, who asked if he had seen or heard anything the night he disappeared.

'No, I'm sorry,' he had replied, telling him that he fell asleep quite early that night and slept until seven or so the next morning.

After their conversation, a creeping anxiety swept over the old man. Could there have been any surveillance cameras that captured what happened? He then walked all over the area, checking all conceivable places where a camera might have been placed and angled toward them. Thankfully, he couldn't find a single camera anywhere; the only ones he saw were two inside some of the shops surrounding the square. These, however, were concentrated on observing the store's merchandise, not what was happening outside.

The search for the missing teen continued, but as with anything, the coverage diminished over time, and two weeks after the initial news article, it was a thing of the past. There was speculation that he had run away from home or taken his own life, but no one ultimately knew where he could be. The search continued, apparently, but when a person wasn't found after a week, the resources poured into that project began to vanish. Things slowly began moving back to normal in Drøbak; It's funny how quickly people adapt and forget about something that was the focal point of all chatter and conversations only weeks ago.

6

The next week at school was difficult for August. His concentration nearly abandoned him completely, and as the week stretched out, chatter about Mathias' disappearance increased exponentially. At first, some of Mathias' friends found it odd he didn't show up at school or participate in their online group chat. It worsened as they tried to get ahold of him without any luck.

'Perhaps he's been hospitalized or something,' Robert, a friend of theirs, remarked. But that theory was quickly scrapped when Mathias' parents began reaching out to every one of his friends, wondering if they had seen him or if he was staying at their place by chance. A grave panic developed in August in anticipation of Mathias' parents reaching out; he didn't know what to say or if he would be able to say anything.

Conversations kept creeping onto the topic of his disappearance; it didn't matter who he talked to. He felt antsy about the idea of having to speak of it and continually dreaded the moment the theme inevitably came up. He didn't know how he would handle it, how to act without raising suspicion.

Thankfully, his friends seemed a little apprehensive to talk about it. They were having lunch when one of his friends, Erik, brought the topic up.

'I keep thinking about his parents and his little brother. God, it must be devastating.'

'Yeah, it's horrible.'

'What do you think happened? And you were the last person to see him, right?'

'Yeah, I think so, but who knows where he went after we hung out? I've no idea what happened; I hope he'll be home any day now.'

'Yeah, I hope so too. But it's strange, isn't it? The whole thing is so weird, and it's not like Mathias to drop off the face of the earth.'

'I know, I don't understand it. I'm afraid something bad has happened, but I hate thinking about it.'

'I understand. I'm sorry. If I had to guess, I think he must have gotten into a fight and was killed by that old bum. That man always gave me the creeps. I'm sure there's an angry and spiteful man hiding behind that dull façade of his. Perhaps he whacked him out of spite.'

'Who knows?'

August felt relieved to hear from one person who didn't seem to place any suspicion at his feet. Despite this, that he had been the last person to see him caused him tremendous worry. It is the last person you hope to be if you have anything to hide; being the last one to see a missing person is never a great sign. The only thing that could make it worse would be a clear motive for murder, jealousy, for instance. It didn't take a very talented artist to paint August as a great suspect. It was the first time the two had spent time together by themselves since Josephine had drastically changed her preference.

At school, he felt a general aversion growing amongst his peers. Eyes would seldom meet his, and when they did, they weren't friendly gazes. Invitations to join others' groups for school projects and casual conversation grew sparse and far between.

A group of students had gone to the principal demanding they expel August. He made them feel unsafe to be at school. *Forced to walk the halls with a killer,* was allegedly what they had said. He wasn't a killer in any judicial sense, but that didn't matter. The thought that he might be a murderer was apparently too uncomfortable. August was told the story by Daniel, another one of his friends, as his little sister was one of those students.

Naive little shits, the friend had branded them, as he recounted the story before August and his friends. Tears pressed forth in August as the story unraveled, yet he tried to appear unbothered. He retorted with empty phrases like 'so dumb' and 'I couldn't care less,' yet the delivery was unconvincing. He couldn't have been more bothered and quickly excused himself from the situation to save what little face remained. Instead of hitching a ride with a friend or the bus, he walked home from school that day. His head hung low, and tears welled forth all of the forty minutes it took to walk home. He felt deflated and shameful.

The next day at school he walked past a group of girls during break. One of the girls, Hannah was her name, a decent-looking girl with red hair and freckles, motioned towards August as the word *murderer* formed unmistakenly on her lips. A helpless rage surged forth in him and he wanted nothing more than to walk up to that pitiful girl, slap her red face, and bring her up against the wall with his hands wrapped around her thin freckled neck. Instead, he navigated straight to the closest bathroom stalls. He remained there for ten minutes, attempting to collect his senses, which was unsuccessful, so he stormed out of school early.

This wasn't sustainable; the life he was leading wasn't worth a dime, it made him resent life. He reflected on these things as he wandered endlessly around Drøbak. Cutting school was necessary today, he thought, as he couldn't bring himself to continue classes after that cruel girl desecrated him. Of course, she didn't really, as she was completely correct in calling him a murderer: that was exactly what he was, yet he was unwilling to accept that.

No, he was no murderer; unlucky and unfortunate, yes. But not a killer. What the hell was he to do? He dreaded going to school and he hated spending time with his parents. They had an image of who he was, but he differed vastly from their perception, so astronomically disproportionate that August felt it appalling to share their space.

It was hell. The only time he had a semblance of peace was by himself in his bedroom. *But what kind of life is that*, he asked himself, staying all day in your room, isolated from the world? And even this little speck of time he had been able to carve out, his parents toiled to dismember, probably motivated by a worry of his wellbeing. Couldn't they tell he needed it? At the end of that day, he lay spread out on his bed with one question in mind: *How do I possibly move forward?*

It was Thursday afternoon when August received a phone call. He sensed it had to be them, so he excused himself from the history class he was attending and stepped into the empty hallway.

'Hello, it's August.'

'It's Mari. Look, August, we don't know where Mathias is. He didn't come home Saturday evening, and we're growing extremely worried that something has happened to our little boy.'

He could hear she was on the verge of crying. The line went silent for a moment, then she continued, 'Do you have any idea where he might be? I beg you, please tell us.'

'I'm so sorry; I have no idea where he is. We did hang out on Saturday even—'

'You saw him on Saturday?!' she burst out, interrupting him mid-sentence.

'Yes,' he said with a low voice. 'We had some beers together by the harbor that evening; it was a good time.

We stayed there until it was dark. That's when I went home and I haven't seen or heard from him since.'

He could hear her panting voice on the other line. 'Jesus, August! You are the last person that saw him that day. How did he seem to you? Did he tell you where he was going after? Is there anything you can tell us that might help?'

'I don't think so, I'm sorry. The only thing I remember was glancing back at him as I started walking home. I saw him walking in the opposite direction of me, which was strange. I mean, we live in the same direction, but I figured he must have been heading to some other place. Josephine's maybe.'

'And you said he hasn't tried to reach you since that evening?'

'No, sorry.'

'Thank you for telling us, August. It means a lot, I'll tell the police that are helping us locate him, what you told me. They might want to speak to you, okay?'

'Of course. I better get back to class now, but I hope he'll be back soon.'

'Mhm, yes, we'll speak.'

'Goodbye.'

Those last few words felt bitter in August's mouth. After hanging up, he stumbled over to a stool and sat down. A dark pit had formed in his bosom as the call went on. It was weighing down on him heavily now, making it difficult to draw a breath. He wondered what would happen now; how long would they be searching for that poor guy?

The best-case scenario, he figured, would be them searching for a few more weeks without finding him; then they would have to search less and less before abandoning it altogether. Without a body, it would be impossible to say what happened. 'I just have to stay sane and retain my normality and innocence no matter what,' he told himself, knowing full well that being the last person who saw Mathias was a horrid situation. He had considered not telling them about their meeting, but he was afraid someone else would reveal it, which would have been catastrophic. He had stupidly told his mother and friends where he had been that evening, so there was little room for deception.

A feeling of nausea began rising in the hopeless man, and he ran to the bathroom to release the tension. Afterward he splashed his red face with water, rinsed his mouth, and slapped both cheeks hard before heading back to class.

During the first period the following day, August's year was told that police would come by the school next week to talk to the students that might know something about Mathias' disappearance. August was sitting in math class when the teacher told them she had a small announcement before class began. Anxiety gripped its cold hands around his neck as the word *police* left his teacher's mouth.

Of course, he knew that they had be looking for Mathias, but somehow he hadn't realized the seriousness of the situation; he would have to face and lie to the police. They would want to speak to him, as he was one of Mathias' friends. After the phone call with Mari, they would surely point to him as the most important person to interrogate.

He wasn't able to concentrate at all in class, and all he wanted to do was to go home and lie in his bed. Yet, he was afraid it would raise suspicion, and so he attempted to remain tranquil, going about the day as normal. It wasn't easy, and the dread of talking to the police became more real and painful as the minutes passed. A slight fever began developing in August, which didn't leave him for several weeks. Towards the end of the day, all the school could talk about was the disappearance of Mathias.

To make things worse, his parents had contacted the national newspapers about his disappearance hoping to get tips; an article had been printed in Aftenbladet, one of Norway's premier newspapers and August's father's favorite. These forces culminated in tremendous discomfort in the young man. The uneasiness began manifesting in physiological twitches in his right hand, and his thoughts started turning erratic and difficult to control.

'I can't go on like this. Breaking one of my stupid rules won't hurt. I'll speak to Rickard tonight,' he concluded when he arrived home.

That night he did go and see Rickard in the hope that he might provide some sound advice and to simply share a space with someone that knew the horrid sides of him. Something was comforting in spending time with a man who knew his darkness and accepted, even loved him, despite it. He had been helpful before, so why not once more?

Their meeting has been recounted, so we won't go into that, but as he left the old man that night, he felt a little more confident he could stand firmly in all the unmistakable difficulties that lay before him.

7

The amount of pitiless and hopeless souls holding onto existence out of habit and fear is saddening. Step into a metro station in any major city at nine pm on a Saturday. These are the invisibles that creep out of their dark caves once or twice a week. They will not be seen during the daytime, but need some fresh air and arousal sporadically. The despair in their eyes is taxing. You don't want to acknowledge their existence. Yet your will doesn't change a thing. Here they still are, drunk and high. Yes, anything to numb the pain that is life.

How did we forsake our brothers and sisters? Our willful ignorance of this subset of the population wears on the souls of all nations that allow it. Most people, it is true, have more than enough with staying alive and sustaining their families. There are also many with ample free time and little material worries. They prance around in a cushy life, never having to commit to anything, which is why they remain nothing.

Or maybe some people are doomed in this world of ours. If you have many eccentric qualities and you can't find a career in the arts, it seems almost inescapable that you will lead a life propped up by social benefits and colored by dread — that is, if you are lucky. One begins to wonder, what causes this? Is it really the fruits of a dysfunctional society? Do some unfortunate spirits possess them, or is it due to actions in past lives? Maybe they raped some helpless woman, which is why they are trapped in this thankless life.

An interesting question then emerges: if these people were presented with a montage of what their lives would look like, would they still take it? The alternative being non-being? It is difficult to say, because despite all the shame and negative emotions, there still would be moments of bliss. Moments of ecstasy. Unfortunately, they would not be a result of an aligned life, but bliss nonetheless would be part of the story that is their lives.

These ideas had plagued Rickard's slumber for years upon years. One evening, while talking to August, he brought up the topic to reveal aspects of life to him and was also curious to see his reaction and thoughts.

'Have you ever seen a drug addict or someone really struggling?'

'Sure, a few times. It was mostly in Oslo, and it broke my heart. I find it difficult to meet their eyes whenever I see those people. And when I look away, I feel guilty for not recognizing their humanity. As if I'm scared that their troubles will contaminate me or something. I don't know exactly.'

'What do you think brought them to that place?'

'Oh, I don't know. I imagine there are as many explanations as there are people.'

'Yeah, that could very well be. Have you actually heard of karmic law?'

'Yes and no, I have heard it before, but I don't really know what it means. Isn't it something like people develop good karma if they behave well and vice versa?'

'Not wrong; in simple terms, it's a law of cause and effect. Everything that happens has a cause, which seems sensible. Where it gets interesting is that in the Indian tradition, they have this notion of reincarnation. That means that you carry the consequences of actions from your previous lives. In their worldview, it explains the incredible inequalities we see in the world.'

'But that's absurd, surely you don't believe in reincarnation?'

'Oh, I don't know. I've heard of worse ideas. I read a book a long time ago; I think it was called *Twenty-five Cases of…* or was it twenty? Yes, *Twenty Cases of Reincarnation* by a fellow called Ian Stevenson. I mean, when you see all the inequality in the world, doesn't it make you wonder?'

'It makes me think the world is unfair, but it doesn't go further than that.'

'Why is that?'

'I am not sure there needs to be a *why*. Maybe it simply is, which is why I find this whole notion of an all-loving God ridiculous.'

'I completely get it. Although I have to say, in my mind, it is simply too absurd to think that all of this came out of nothing. I have the sense that there is some underlying creative force at play.'

'I don't think that sounds too unreasonable, but I don't think much about those things, to tell you the truth. I have enough things to attend to in my life at the moment, maybe even a little too much,' he said, followed by a good chuckle.

They both smiled, but Rickard didn't feel he had gotten any closer to the truth of his conundrum. August was too immature for now, so he felt pleased at planting this idea of a creative force in him. Not because he wanted to convince him of anything, but in the hopes that he would have to contend with the idea and find out what he thought. Having an idea of the metaphysics of the universe is fruitful, lest one sleepwalks throughout the whole of life. Bearing a conscious thought about how the universe might function definitively shapes how you relate to the world and other people.

Rickard wondered what he could have been up to in his previous lives to be leading the life he did now. It couldn't have been too honorable, given he was homeless now. Then again, that was somewhat his own choice. A choice that followed with a lot of baggage. Had he been wired differently, he could be a *normal* functioning person. Content with some useless job, perpetually filling the gaps in his life with new stuff, sitting in a comfortable home and watching endless television in his spare time. In some ways, it would be a better life, simply due to the ignorance of it all. Much easier. It was way too late for that; he had seen too much and understood the universe a little too well to fall into that trap. He didn't know much, but enough not to go down that path. Although he didn't know why and how, he knew there was an untold significance to existence. He had found a way of honoring that, in part, through an Eastern way of life. There had been a remarkable change in his being, as he slowly aligned parts of himself. It was obvious that this change of lifestyle was right. It was true. Hence, that common path of the eroded soul and empty existence in modern society wasn't appealing to the old man.

One might reasonably ask why many people choose just that road, then. To some degree, it is the cultural blueprint laid out, although it's by no means the only one. There is no doubt that it is a productive path. In the service of technological and humanitarian progress, it makes sense. Under capitalism, living standards have increased to an unfathomable degree. That is important. But is life all about a higher living standard? Surely, there is a greater quest in life than raising the standards of life and increasing the gross domestic product of your nation? Rickard thought the issue with these goals and ideals was that they spoke to a shallow, almost external part of life. There was no depth, no spirit in these endeavors. There was no poetry or beauty in any of that. The depth of the human experience has all but lost its meaning and significance these days. A melancholy brewed in Rickard's being as he mulled these thoughts repeatedly, resting on Abraham in the evenings. He had found his own way to a richness that he didn't believe existed in the first half of his life. An inner richness that spilled out, coloring his experience in myriad ways. It took cultivation and exploration to get there. It also took tremendous sacrifice. He had to let go of the life he thought he needed to lead, and his whole identity was tied up with those ideas. It is no easy feat to untie his thwarted destiny from all those powerful knots.

Maybe he was a madman; anyone speaking of a deep well within will be dismissed or branded a romantic in the best-case scenario. If you are an old, untidy man as well, you can receive poor treatment. So Rickard usually kept these thoughts to himself, although they would spill out in small ways during conversation. He enjoyed speaking to people. He found people to be mysteries walking, so any opportunity was met with joy. Yet, he felt shy at times, and the judgement thrown at him was painful. Rising above that proved difficult for Rickard, and not for a lack of effort. But that is the issue; the striving for this mode of being is fruitless. No striving or effort can bring you there. A blessing seems to be required, although certain steps can be taken to increase the likelihood of being blessed.

8

It was early morning when August stepped down the stairs to have breakfast. His mother was already standing in the kitchen, fixing the morning coffee.

'Good morning, darling. Do you mind running by the bakery to pick up some bread and those Danish pastries I adore?'

'Sure.'

'Thank you. Want some coffee?'

'Yes, thanks.'

She poured a cup for herself and one for August, placing them both on the kitchen island. She looked cautiously at him, sensing some overbearing shadow lingering upon her son.

'How are you feeling?' she said.

'I'm fine,' he retorted dryly.

She moved a little closer to her son. 'Are you sure? You don't seem like yourself, as if something is weighing on you.'

Her look of concern turned into a sly smile. 'Love perhaps?'

'No, stop, will you? There's nothing; I just had a poor night of sleep. I'm tired, that's all.' He lowered his gaze, as it felt too painful to behold her prying eyes.

'Do you have any plans for the day?' he continued, forcing a smile.

'Yes!' she said merrily. 'Your father and I are heading to this cute little place twenty minutes from here. It's this outside area with a small vegetable garden and some free-roaming animals, and there's this wonderful little café there. Jenny from work suggested it; she was there the other day and adored it!'

'Sounds lovely!'

'You are welcome to join us,' she replied enthusiastically.

'Thank you, but I'll have to pass. I look forward to hearing about it later, though. I might head to the park with some friends. Anyhow, I should get going. Is the old man still sleeping?' She nodded, causing them both to grin.

'I'll take the car, see you soon,' he said before throwing the remains of the cup down the hatch.

The sun had peered over the horizon a while ago when August brought the weary tires of his mother's car onto the road. The sky was China blue, and the magnificent morning presented a picture-perfect opposite of August's internal landscape. As he sat there ruminating behind the wheel, an oppressive discomfort enveloped him, giving no sign of easing its grip. The feeling had first arrived a week ago. He had hoped it would diminish over time, but it didn't subside for a moment.

There was a common parking lot in the city. August left the car there, taking up one of a sea of free lots scattered about. Most people seemed to be home on this fine Sunday morning, likely breaking bread and sharing laughs, he thought. He wondered whether he could ever experience those simple joys once more; these were painful thoughts, as he feared he might never have that chance again. *But time heals all wounds*, right? Maybe all that was needed was a little less cynicism and letting the relentless stream of time wash away the painful memories.

The bell above the entrance door rang out as he entered the bakery, causing Tom's head to shoot up from behind the counter.

'Morning, August! How is my favorite thug?'

August looked bewildered. 'What do you mean, thug?' he answered uneasily.

'Hah, I'm messing with you. How's it going?'

'Ah, yeah I'm okay. And you?'

'Every day as a free man is a blessed day,' he said with a thin smile. 'Did your mother send you again? Is she scared to come herself, afraid she can't help herself?'

'She sure did. Can you just give me some sourdough bread and a handful of those pastries over there?'

'Of course, coming right up. And hey, I'm just joking around'

'I know, I know. I've just had a horrible night's sleep. I'm in no mood.'

As the baker gathered up the requested items in a bag, August's mind wandered back to the unfortunate night. 'What did I hope to gain from it? Why the hell did I invite him at all. If only I could go back and restrain my stupid self. Ah god, all that fucking chaos from a puny punch.'

'Do you know that boy that's gone missing? Real tragedy, that whole situation. I hope he pops back up someplace soon.'

August was struck by the untimely question, given he had been replaying his killing a second ago. He couldn't get a word out, so he stood there dumb and mute.

'Hey, I'm sorry again. That was insensitive of me. Of course you know him; he's right around your age. Hell, I even think I've seen the two of you walking about. Were you close?'

The question made him feel anxious, and he wondered if he was alluding to something, but by some miracle he nodded calmly before continuing:

'Yes, he was one of… I mean, he is one of my good friends.'

Tom looked suspiciously at him, and then smiled meekly. A smile that felt like a monstrous boulder rolling on top of August's neck and shoulders. The baker placed a large paper bag on the counter.

'That'll be 180 kroner.'

August fished out his mother's credit card and paid as fast as he could muster. God forbid he had to stay in that wretched place a second more than needed. He didn't dare look back at Tom's peering eyes. He must suspect me, but how? What could have caused him to act like that, trying to lure things out of me? August entertained the terrifying thought that he could have seen them on the night of the murder. But that was unlikely; he would have told the police by now, and he would already have been in unimaginable trouble. Maybe he had seen them walking together toward the city from his apartment window. Yes, he thought, he didn't know exactly what happened but he seemed to know something had happened. The unknowable nature of Tom's suspicions caused a worsening anxiety in the young man. On the drive home, he couldn't rid himself of the fear that this bloody baker would cause him tremendous trouble.

As the young man rushed out the door, Tom stood thinking about the young man's odd behavior. His reaction reminded him of a painful experience that inevitably led to his imprisonment decades ago. A *faithful* friend of his, who had full knowledge of his criminal activities, had also acted very strange in the face of normal questions; August's demeanor had touched a pattern he had seen in that man all those years ago.

They both shared a peculiar look that, in Tom's eyes, revealed a startled fear of being put to death. Going mute was another sign that the mind was scrambling to find the proper words for the lie. When one speaks the truth, it is easy. Although it may hurt, it doesn't strain the mind the way a lie will. Well, at least not for the untrained liar—which is most of us.

Then he remembered that Rickard brought the name of that boy up, unprompted, when they spoke of the missing kid. That seemed like a strange coincidence too, he thought. Yes, there was no doubt something unsavory going on here. Maybe that was what had caused him to tease August when he walked in. Maybe a part of him wanted to rouse the young man, to see whether there was anything to be found there, beneath the surface.

9

The season shifted from early summer into a mature one, evident by the delightful morning air and earthy dusk of the fresh green leaves. Down the main street from the square of Drøbak, you would find a hairdresser named Azur run by a stern and judicial woman. On the floor above, there was a little apartment of about forty square meters. It was occupied by Thomas Bankran, the local baker in town who'd opened up his little shop several years ago.

'Good morning, old man.'

'Morning, Tom!'

'How's it going?'

'Well, the sun's shining, and the birds are chirping. It doesn't get better than that, does it?'

'I suppose you're right about that, but how about that poor kid, huh? I wonder what happened to him.'

'God only knows.'

'Haha, yes, maybe. Although I suspect one or two others are also in on it with good old God there.'

'Hehe, who knows! Anyhow, has anything new happened since last?'

'Yes, in fact! Funny that you ask, I met a kind young lady the other day. Kirsten was her name. Yeah, we spent time together this weekend. She's a real treat, that girl,' Tom said with a big smile.

'Good,' he said, 'and what deliciousness have you crafted for us this morning?' His gaze fell on the display of pastries relaxing before him behind a thick pane of glass.

'Same old. Same old,' he answered, looking blankly right through Rickard. Probably thinking about that woman, Rickard surmised. Suddenly, the liveliness returned to Tom's eyes. 'A Drøbak bread and a Danish pastry as usual?'

'Just the bread this time; I'll keep the pastry for another time.'

'That's a first!'

'Not good for the body, I hear.'

'Hah! That never stopped you before. What's up? Are you short on money? Hell, I'll throw it in for free, Rickard.'

'No, no. That's kind, Tom. I just don't feel like it today. Something, that lost kid perhaps, is disturbing my appetite.'

'Alright then,' he said before grabbing a freshly baked bread from the shelf behind him and sliding it into a thin brown paper bag.

A whiff of vanilla traveled around the room of the little establishment, which was neat and small. The pastries seemed to stretch out their arms at one, like little orphans, begging you to bring them home. Thomas had learned the art of baking over many years, and by now one was tempted to call him a master of the trade; of course, he would never admit to that, being somewhat humble in his professional disposition.

'Thank you. I hope you have a busy day ahead!'

'Thanks!' he replied, giving a gentle nod to the old man. However, as he was headed out the door, the baker shouted, 'Hey, Rickard! Come by at the end of the day. We'll share some coffee or beers out front here, alright?'

'Sounds lovely, see you later.'

Rickard enjoyed the companionship of this rugged baker, although he didn't particularly enjoy his personhood. He was a little too extravagant and excitable than the people Rickard usually preferred. Tom was a renowned man for all the wrong reasons: a reformed criminal and a serial womanizer. Rickard always tried to withhold judgment about any man or lifestyle, yet it wasn't easy with this fellow. At times, he had found the way he described his encounters with women unsavory to the point of despair. For all the gifts he had been endowed with, social awareness or a filter was not one of them. At one point, he recounted an story to Rickard that went something like this:

'We were fondling around on the couch. Passionately, I tell you. And we were buzzed up to the gills with delightful Amarone, and this woman was as sexy as can be. Eventually, she slides off the couch and onto her knees. She gripped my shaft with both hands and went to work with her chapped lips. One of her hands even slid off and ended up between her legs. She went on like that for a few minutes when, wouldn't you know it, her damn husband barged through the front door. He was standing there with grocery bags and their two children. Unfortunately, I locked eyes with the poor chap as he walked in. The entrance door could be seen from a side angle of the living room, you see. Safe to say it was a small house. The ideal scenario would have been a bigger house, where the living room was hidden upon arrival.

Then, maybe I could have gotten the hell out before chaos ensued. Or maybe not, who knows? Haha!

'Anyway, the poor bastard looked like that fellow in Munch's famous painting. The grocery bags dropped to the floor, and he attempted to cover the eyes of his children in vain. He went quiet for a good ten seconds, then a shrill voice exclaimed, "Get out! Go, get the hell out, and stay by the car!"

'The bitch was still on her knees with her head planted in my lap, frozen with shame, I imagine. She was probably hoping it was all one of those horrid dreams, waiting hopefully for the veil to be torn to the side, and to wake up covered by her velvet sheets. Funnily enough, I found the whole situation very arousing. I contemplated tugging at it, as I was already near fulfillment, but decided against it. I gently pushed her face off and back, kissed her on the cheek, then I whispered, "Good luck, darling."

'I threw my clothes on, and I got out of there. On the way out, I shook the man's hand. Hah! The dumbo simply stood there. What an experience!'

Tom had gleefully recounted this story, where any decent man would surely keep it to himself or, perhaps more accurately, would've never found himself in that situation. The only redeeming part of that story was that he did mention feeling bad for the husband, but that only occurred a while after he had told the tale. The pride and gleefulness had to settle a little first, he figured. The man had some type of conscience, but it was a frail and malnourished little thing.

Despite this, he was a kind and good-humored man. Just about the same time Rickard arrived in Drøbak all those years ago, Tom had rented a locale in the city. Much like Rickard, he was an outsider to the town and hence didn't receive a very warm welcome. His somewhat rough look didn't scream mild manners or tranquility, which caused a general aversion to the man. They found company in each other when the rest of the city was uninterested in engaging with them much. However, as people realized who Tom was before his arrival, his popularity grew. There is something alluring about a reformed person, a man capable of doing things we normal people would only dream of, who now walks among us like a normal citizen. By rubbing shoulders with those people, we imagine we might catch something of their unsanctioned wildness. The wildness we all possess as children that is carved out of us in the grand process of socialization.

Rickard however did not experience any growth in popularity, as one would expect with a slightly deranged homeless man. So, he stayed in the background with an undeveloped social circle, whilst Tom was warmly embraced by the little town. Although Tom had to peer far down from his spot on the hierarchical ladder to see Rickard, it didn't deter him from occasionally talking to the old man, whom he found amusing and strange.

Rickard spent the day walking about the woods. Little birds sang their hearts out, bouncing from branch to branch, while he sang happily along. The woods were mostly empty during the weekdays; hence, he gravitated toward them. He enjoyed strolling along the thin pathways laid about. He even liked creating new ones, which was often more troublesome than joyful, but that didn't stop the stubborn old man. His trustworthy traveling companion, the book, was also slid out of his blazer pocket, where it always rested, a few times that day.

He stopped before a pond, contemplating taking a little bath; it had been some time since he had showered, so it wasn't a bad idea. But he had forgotten to bring a towel along, so he decided against it. He made do by removing his top, splashing some fresh water beneath his armpits, and refreshing his hairy face. The cold sensation of water on his face was delightful, making him feel refreshed and alive.

As the day dragged on and the sun galloped further and further westward, he realized it was probably nearing the closing time of Tom's shop, so he began heading toward the city, taking his time. He was never in a hurry, and hadn't been for years. His ideas about time had changed dramatically over the last decades. Time is treated like a god nowadays, and people's lives are utterly bound up with the time of day. We are happy slaves to our construct, albeit a very useful construct for productivity. His relationship with time these days was an unserious one, much like a relationship with a mistress: not of primary concern, yet you still care about her and attempt to keep a functional relationship with her to prevent your life from falling apart.

When Rickard arrived at Tom's bakery, he was sitting outside on a little Parisian bench he had proudly acquired. He sipped his glass-bottled Peroni, with five more bottles in a little cardboard box beside him. Rickard sat down, thanking Tom for the invitation, and they began exchanging stories and laughs.

‘Every wicked notion throws a beautiful shadow,’ said Tom as his gaze rested calmly on the clouds above. ‘You’re not allowed one without the other, just as well as you can’t produce a child by yourself.’

‘That all depends on whose glasses you’re peering through,’ replied Rickard before taking a generous sip of the beer graciously given to him.

‘How the hell is that?’

‘Well, it’s a little difficult to put it forth directly. Perhaps indirectly will do. Mind if I share a little story?’

‘Go for it.’

Rickard closed his tired eyes and worked to bring the little story together from fragments of his mind. He shifted a little on the bench they were sitting on, then he opened his eyes and said, ‘A group of men, four I think it was, were taking a little evening stroll in the nearby forest one warm evening many years ago. They were right outside their little village, situated south of West Bengal in India. A wise old man led the group, while the other three were blind young men. Suddenly, the group stumbled upon an elephant! The animal seemed curious, as it approached the group graciously before coming to a dead halt before the three young men.

"What is that before you?" asked the wise old man, and the men reached out, trying to determine what it could be.

"It's a rope!" proclaimed the first man.

"Are you dumb? It's clearly a tree trunk," said the second.

"You blind fools, can you tell it's a mud wall?"

The men went on arguing for a while, each convinced they were right. Eventually, the old man butted in.

"You've all got it wrong. All of you are touching only a part of the whole; that is what's getting you all mixed up. This, my dear friends, is an elephant, and it's both all of these things and none of them."

Tom looked perplexed and stayed silent. His faculties had difficulties wrapping themselves around the elegant little tale.

'Who wrote that?' he asked.

'I think a better question is who came up with that, because I'm sure this story came into being long before writing burst onto the scene, but God only knows. All I can tell you is that it is a story from the East.'

Tom's unsettled face turned into a grin. 'You do know how to tell a good story, don't you, Rickard?'

'It's a simple and powerful tale, I think—the way stories ought to be.'

'You're right. I don't know if I fully get it, but you've given me something to think about. No doubt about it.'

'Good,' he replied with a warm smile.

They continued drinking their beers and talking jovially until the exhausted sun hid behind the short houses of Storgata. Rickard, too, was sleepy and looked forward to his slumber. The streets of Drøbak were quiet by now, and people were mostly gathered in their homes, enjoying supper amongst each other or cradling before the black box of dull entertainment. The two men shared each other's company, but that was enough. They enjoyed each other tremendously, partly because they had both lived their fair share of life.

It can be a dreary experience, this life. But even worse is spending time with someone who can't comprehend your worldview or experiences. This is one of the reasons class differences are so pervasive and will continue to be, as it's unbearable to spend time with unrelatable humans. Spending time alone is much preferred to spending time with someone where you feel alone. Yes, that's almost a sin, which is why it is experienced as so insufferable. At least being alone affords one calmness, clarity, and room to be oneself. When one spends time with another, one is obliged to wear a costume called *socialized personality*, which represents a relation to who one is. Yet, the degree to which one feels comfortable being oneself depends entirely on the person one is around and, to some degree, on one's self-confidence. That means how much one needs to put on the various parts of our societal customs depends on the trust and relatability of the person one interacts with. The ideal of love is finding a person before whom you can stand stark naked.

10

August's erratic thoughts didn't leave him despite the days moving stubbornly along. His main worry, as he would be speaking to the police soon, was whether they could pick up on his deception. He had never enjoyed lying, and so naturally he wasn't very good at it. As his life hung in the balance, he hoped that would yield some organic motivation. Thankfully, he wasn't mistaken, as a surge of revivifying energy of calm and confidence streamed forth as he took a seat before an officer that following Monday at 10:30.

'Hi August, my name is Johannes. Thank you for taking the time.' He shifted around his seat, looking slightly uncomfortable. 'We won't be long; I know you have classes to attend. However, we're looking at something severe today, and anything you tell us can prove helpful in locating your friend, Mathias. I understand from Mari that you saw him the evening of his disappearance?'

'Yes, that's right.'

'Okay,' the officer said before pausing for a few seconds. He stared intensively at August. 'Did anything happen that evening?'

The question made his throat itch as droplets of sweat began watering his temples. 'Nothing special, like I told Mari. We just hung out drinking a few beers,' he said. The sentence felt artificial to him as it left his lips causing him to feel queasy. The man, he felt, didn't look convinced at all. The officer continued asking an array of questions, which August tried to answer as truthfully as he could. He made him recount every detail of the evening. However, it didn't take much more than fifteen minutes before the man thanked August for his time, and the young man strolled out of the empty classroom. Leaving the room, he felt a mixture of confusion and elation. He was worried about what the takeaway would be for the officer. *Could he be thinking I killed Mathias right now?* flickered through his mind, as a slight terror mounted. Counterbalancing this was the ecstatic joy of having escaped that dreadful room.

Outside the classroom, sequestered by the police for interviews, he saw Josephine sitting on a chair, presumably waiting to be called in. She looked beautiful, he thought, although the whole situation had visibly taken a toll on her; she had heavy eyes cradled by darkened rings and thin red lines running down her cheeks. Seeing her stirred August's heart; he was glad to see her, yet the obvious pain she was carrying around was all his fault. She didn't notice August coming out of the room, as she was preoccupied with her eyes fixed on her shoes. He wanted to say something. Anything. But he couldn't and slipped down the hall unnoticed by the woman his heart belonged to; love will play many cruel tricks on you, the worst being unrequited love.

August was once again going by the bakery to pick up their usual order. The last time he had been there, Tom had been pulling his leg forcefully, so he was trying to enter with the right state of mind: humorous, to the degree he could muster, anyway. He was afraid of alerting Tom, as he already sensed he had a hunch about what had happened. The second he stepped into the establishment, they locked eyes. His look was deadly serious, and August's veins filled with ice.

'Listen up, kid, I know something bad happened. I saw it eating away at you last time you were here, and I see it now, still. It's written across your face, for us with eyes to see. I know you're weighing all your options right now, thinking about what to do and where to run when you get the chance. I'm guessing you'll want to run to another city and country when you finish school, to start over. Let me be the first to tell you, that's all a myth—you cannot outrun your conscience. I mean, you've clearly been endowed with one, and no amount of trickery or strategizing will make it otherwise.' He paused while lowering his gaze with pursed lips.

'You see, what we all truly need and want is a heart at ease, a peaceful abode for the center of our being. I'm sorry to tell you this, but that is an experience you'll be lacking until you own up to whatever it is that you know you need to.'

August's body had started shaking while Tom was speaking; his hands twitched and his teeth clattered. How could he know? Why would he tell him this instead of handing him over to the cops? Did he really know? A thousand thoughts ran through his mind, latching onto every word spoken. Yes, he wasn't sure exactly of what had happened, but that something did was unquestionable. August crumbled onto himself and felt smaller than ever before.

'What I've done is inexcusable,' he mumbled beneath his breath. He was shocked at himself for giving it all up so easily. All those rules and ideas about how he would act were thrown out the minute someone confronted him.

'There is no such thing. Your heart doesn't care about the severity of your sins; it's intelligent enough to know it's too late for that. What matters now is how you act after the fact.'

Later that week, sitting at the breakfast table with his parents, his mother got word from a friend that an unidentified body had washed up on a beach. The body had been discovered early that morning by joggers, and soon, the police had sectioned off the area. August nearly fell into a nervous breakdown upon hearing this; his thoughts were scattered all over the place, and he could not sit still. He gave some lame excuse about forgetting a meet-up with a friend and stormed out of the house.

The moment he'd feared beyond belief was here, and he wasn't surprised. From the moment Mathias' head hit the cobblestoned ground, a part of him knew there was only a matter of time before it would be discovered. All would be revealed. The whole ordeal even caused a little relief, as the continuous fear of the body being discovered at any time was killing him. Overpowering the positive emotion of relief, however, was the despairing fact that he was in deadly trouble. Before one might have been charmed by the theory that Mathias had run away. That tale was long gone now, as he lay there, like a ghost on the wet sand. August was the last person to see him; everyone knew that by now, and so he would be the prime suspect.

August took to the woods, not knowing where to go. The question he had asked himself earlier, *how the hell do I move forward*, kept ringing through his mind as he traversed up to the highest point of Drøbak. It was a small stone peak, scattered with pine trees, overlooking the Oslofjord. When he finally reached the top, he felt winded and sat down. His eyes peered across the water as he weighed the paths forward.

One solution was to run away. To buy a one-way ticket to some distant country, and start his life all over. Preferably to some country without an extradition agreement with Norway. There must be plenty of those, he figured. He was eighteen and would surely manage to get by somehow. To start over and create another life—it didn't sound so bad. But he would have to leave now, before becoming a suspect, whence he would be placed on some no-fly list. The remaining two options were to give in or to continue fighting.

He was confused; all the options sounded equally terrible. He closed his eyes. The gentle breeze kissed his strained face as August let go of his mind, simply allowing his feelings and thoughts to flow as they wished.

It was a pain unlike any other, the dreadful realization that he had dug his own grave; the rest of his life would be ridden with dread, pain and isolation.

'Unless...' a little voice whispered, almost unintelligibly, from the deepest recesses of his mind. He focused on this voice, eager to hear its plea. 'Unless you stand firm and retain your innocence. It may play out favorably; you might regain your freedom.'

'Why yes, of course!' he exclaimed with troubling laughter.

Sitting on top of Drøbak's tallest mountain, a veil of serenity fell upon his being, and a spark of hope was ignited in his bosom. There was no evidence to tie him to the murder, other than circumstantial, as far as he knew. If only he could remain steadfast in his innocence, there might be a way out of this hell.

11

Rickard learned about the death from Tom, who told him that the body washed up on a local beach near the park. The knot around the dead man's feet had come loose, and he had been carried a few hundred meters north by the currents.

This discovery sent the whole town into a frenzy and caused immense distress for both August and Rickard. Fingers were pointed at many different people, yet a general suspicion grew toward the homeless man, as is often the case with minorities—the outsider is easier to step on, hold down, and blame.

The inhabitants of Drøbak began keeping their children home during the late hours of the evening, and there was a general uneasiness permeating the little town. A shock of this magnitude leaves a mark on an otherwise peaceful small town, a little like a beautiful child from a good home being abused. Everyone is deeply affected and moved by such a happening, which differs greatly from some poor child coming from a broken home being mistreated. That would be like the wicked crimes carried out in large cities every day. One becomes desensitized and apathetic to go on.

There was a vigil held about a month after Mathias's body was found. At 18:00, on a gloomy Thursday, the townsfolk gathered on the city square, where the "kommune", which is the municipality in Norway, had built a shoddy podium. Henrik Langsom, the mayor of Drøbak, was to say a few remarks along with the priest of the local church. Henrik was an indolent and corrupt man, everyone agreed, but he was also jovial and energetic, which almost made up for his shortcomings. He was narrow in a metaphysical sense, yet broad in the physical.

People wondered what he could possibly contribute at this time, but that's the job, isn't it? You show up, wanted or not, and attempt to string together a few sensible words, then retreat to your publicly funded office. The reason everybody knew the man was corrupt was due to his sudden and continued surge in familial wealth, after taking office. He had been a business owner running a carpeting firm, before becoming the mayor. He handed the reins over to his two sons when he stepped into the public domain. The business grew dramatically and branched out into various ventures, alongside Henrik's growing influence. Out of nowhere, projects that had been stalled and stopped for years were being approved by the kommune, when the Langsom boys came knocking. The whole thing was ridiculously blatant, but aside from a few angry inhabitants and columns in the local newspaper, nothing was done.

Perhaps that's just the way it is in most small towns. Corruption is allowed to run up to a certain threshold with nothing happening. People are too busy navigating their own lives, to worry much about people gaming the system a little. The question is when does it go too far? It is difficult to say, but we can say with a certain degree of certainty that it hadn't gone *too* far in Drøbak. Not yet, anyhow.

The priest was also to share some remarks at the vigil. She was an old and charming lady. Rickard had spoken to her occasionally, and she always treated him with warmth. She was well liked by the community, and people were looking forward to her speaking.

A restless fear had gripped the town, and the inhabitants were eager to rid themselves of the unwavering looming skies. Maybe Maria's speech, the name of the priest, would help dim the chaotic undercurrents that ran beneath the small town.

As the time neared the beginning of the vigil, the square was swimming with people, yet voices were low and weary. No laughter nor joy was felt across the cold cobbled stone square. Eyes scattered between quick glances before falling to the ground. Many had felt obligated to show up, but as they stood there, they only felt annoyed at having to waste their time here, wallowing in sadness. Most didn't know the boy well, but their compassion for the poor parents brought them out. 'Imagine if that was your boy?' you would hear people say. Yes, any decent parent would give up all their possessions, life too, to prevent such a happening.

Rickard lingered by the outer ring of the gathered crowd, alongside the people that cared least about the ordeal but didn't have the courage to say *fuck this.* These folks could hardly claim any real virtue, like the rest, but felt too afraid to admit and showcase their carelessness.

'Did you know the kid?' a father queried his teenage daughter.

'No, not really. But I heard he assaulted his girlfriend, so you won't see me shedding any tears.'

Her mother bumped her shoulder with a scornful look, while the father looked somewhat shocked, then shrugged his shoulders and returned his gaze toward the podium where the mayor was about to commence with his opening remarks.

The mayor gripped the podium stand firmly and cleared his throat grotesquely. He wore a dark orange blazer and a tight blue shirt. Rickard thought he resembled a circus director without the extravagant hat. Or maybe he had been dragged out of his weekly poker game with pals, having forgotten all about where he was to perform later.

'Dear inhabitants of Drøbak, my late father always said *the goose may be a darling, but goddamn does she shit*. I never knew exactly what he meant by that, but in my later years I think he was alluding to life and its happenings. As beautiful as it can be, it also carries a tragic side. An incomprehensible side. A wicked thing happened here, in our lovely little town. A father and a mother were robbed of the greatest gift of all. I'm speaking of offspring, of course! They are fun. They are joyous, and what would we do… Hmm, where was I? Apologies, I'm losing my head a little; allow me a moment, would you please?'

He stopped for a few seconds, stepping back and shaking his head lightly. Presumably, it was a strategy to reactivate the thread he had fallen off.

'Ah, yes!' he said lightly. 'The dead boy, now I remember.' This was said beneath his breath, yet the microphone was just able to pick it up and proclaim it to the square. A cry of surprise ran through the crowd, and the mayor flushed as red as a pepper. Before he collapsed altogether, he exclaimed, 'We're all here to cherish the memory of a wonderful boy that was taken from us. Join me all in a minute of silence honoring Mathias's memory.'

The mayor lowered his head and felt prideful that he had salvaged the embarrassing situation from cascading into a catastrophe. During the minute, the mayor's head was seen peering out at the crowd a handful of times to check whether people were complying with his suggestion. It caused a playful humming in Rickard, who felt sorry for the middle-aged man.

The front of the precarious podium was ordained with flowers and big white bows with loving words sewn onto them, and in the midst of it all lay a golden-framed picture of a beautiful young man.

Rickard wondered if August would show up, but he had seen no signs of him. It would probably be better to stay clear, he thought, to keep himself out of potentially compromising situations. Then again, it might also be strange not to show up.

'Thank you all for coming out this evening and taking good care of each other in these troubling times!' said Henrik, before bowing deeply and smiling generously. Then he waltzed off the little stage, and before he had time to settle down on his seat in the front row, an elegant woman trod lightly up toward the podium.

She had angelic blue eyes and the demeanor of a loving grandmother. Her voice was raspy due to a life of smoking.

'Few things are as incomprehensible as youthful death. We say, *damn you, God!* and we would be in the right. Yet, don't forget, we should not pity the dead. God has only gained a worthy companion a little earlier than we would prefer. That is our loss and their gain. Don't despair, we will follow in our own time. I met Mathias many years ago and had the joy of getting to know him while he prepared for his confirmation. He was no doubt a unique boy with the ample gifts of charm and energy.

Yes, he was blessed in many ways, and a single encounter would tell you as much.

All of us standing here today stand together in great love for our late brother. Don't forsake the feeling you all hold in your hearts at this very moment. Let your love flow abundantly forth and share it with your brothers and sisters. Let us all do this, for the sake of Mathias, to play our god-given role in moving our little town closer towards paradise.

'May God bless you. Now, let us pray for Mathias and his family.'

A few people in the crowd were moved to tears and all wrapped their hands together, believers and non-believers alike, pouring their aching love into Mathias, his parents and brother.

Maria walked off the stage and went over to two people that were standing close to the front. She embraced them both, and they both rested their despairing heads on her shoulders.

Rickard felt melancholic that the young man had ripped a hole in their hearts. Nothing would bring their son back, short of a fleeting glimpse of their beloved in a blissful dream. There was a shred of doubt in his heart whether he did the right thing. It might have been better for all, even August, had he helped him turn himself in. He knew that the young man was struggling carrying that horrid event around. It was a secret he needed to carry to death, and who knows what would await him there. Yes, maybe his intuition to help him had been faulty. He looked toward the grieving parents once more, who were sitting huddled on their chairs, with the father holding his wife tightly. Behind them were trees dancing gently in the wind, and the whole square was quiet. He spotted a few seagulls cruising above the treetops—four of them, intermingled and playing. He stood transfixed, beholding the birds dance above them, when someone bumped his shoulder.

'Hey old man!' said a friendly voice.

'Hey you! How's it going?' he replied in a constricted voice, with birds still hovering around in his mind.

'Sad day.'

'Mhm.'

'Are they finished now, or is anyone else supposed to speak?'

'I think they're finished. I enjoyed her little speech.'

'Yeah, she's a fine woman. And priest too,' he replied with a laugh.

Rickard smiled politely, then silence ensued. He turned back toward the podium to see if the birds were still there. Now, there was only the silent sky with a few clouds drifting across the canvas. A nostalgic sensation rose up in his being, but he could not pinpoint the origin. It was an uncanny familiarity with the moment. He figured it was something from his youth trying to push up from his subconscious. He turned back toward the baker, then said,

'Are you up for a walk? I still have my little evening stroll to get through before I retire for the night.'

'Oh, I should be getting back. You are sweet for asking.'

'Very well, have any plans?'

'Uh. I have a thing with a friend later, yeah.'

'Alright, have a nice evening, Tom,' he replied, noting his clunky demeanor. It was obvious he didn't want to be seen walking around with Rickard at this time. He shook his hand, and then he headed for the harbor, as he did every evening.

12

Being the outsider in a small town, where a young man mysteriously dies, is unsurprisingly an unfortunate situation to find oneself in. Rickard felt this firsthand throughout the saga of Mathias' disappearance.

When it became widely known that the young man was missing, suspicions started to mount and build on top of Rickard's poor lot. The first symptom was the dirty looks. Under normal circumstances, people didn't bother Rickard much with their judgmental eyes; the townsfolk had generally grown accustomed to him by now. He had shown over time that he bothered no one, and so people tacitly approved, or at least tolerated, the old man despite his appearance.

The days became harder to carry for the old man, as he began being harassed regularly. The worst, however, he felt, wasn't the pestering but the way people would look at him. Instead of looking at him with pity, they now saw a monster. His troubles grew hand in hand with the contemptuousness amongst Drøbak's inhabitants. It manifested in different ways, one example being that a few bold teenagers began throwing comments at him like 'Murderer!' 'Criminal!'

This felt a little disconcerting to Rickard, but he figured it would blow over. Nobody could know whether he was guilty of anything.

One night he was awakened as someone was rattling around in his suitcase placed in the bushes.

'HEY! What the hell are you doing?' Rickard screamed.

It became quiet, then he saw a shadow hurrying away and out of sight. He went over to the suitcase to evaluate the damages, and the bastard had stolen his remaining beers, on top of having pierced his juice bottle. The perpetrator had also scattered the little food he had around in the dirt. He deeply cursed the fate of the man then he lightly let it go.

Eventually he settled back onto his bench to sleep, but before he traveled back to the world of dreams, he recognized August's steps approaching. He sat up and smiled warmly at the approaching young man. He was glad to see his friend, yet deeply saddened about the troubles he was going through. It was dark, but August's troubles were still clearly seen in his strained face.

'It's good to see you; come take a seat.'

'It's a cruel joke, this life.'

'What makes you say that?'

'Oh, look around! This life I've been given... For what? Now it'll all be taken away, I know it. All over a mishap, a mistake, a terrible, terrible mistake.'

His eyes grew shiny, making them softly reflect the crescent moon in the sky.

'A pitiless existence, worthless. And so very frail!' He paused for a moment. 'God, how frail the whole lot is. Yet we prance around joyfully. Blissfully even. As if a bag is pulled over our heads and we can't see the world for what it is. The noose tightening the bag around our necks must be choking us, because otherwise how could it be that we go on, seemingly unbothered?'

'Listen here, son, you're not wrong. Not entirely anyhow, life is difficult; it's suffering, betrayal, death, and all that—although that's only one side of the coin. We are simple creatures. If ignorance can shield us from much of the horrid elements of life, at least for a while, we suckle at it like newborns.' Rickard went silent, sighing heavily. 'I've been up and down my fair share of valleys in this life. Your misfortune is that all those terrible forces of life have been piled upon you all at once. This, understandably, has given you little chance to comprehend and appreciate the beauty of this world. In the end it's all balanced; there is harmony in this universe, trust me. You'll find it if you search.'

Rickard reached into his left blazer pocket and pulled out a worn-out paperback.

'This proved to be a helpful pillar in my life. A little companion to help peer into reality, to take off that bag you mentioned. It has already served its purpose for me.'

He placed the book in August's lap, who looked down at the cover.

'I've never heard of this book.'

'It was written by a wise man of the East, several millennia ago, that's all you need to know.'

'Okay, I'll take your word for it. Thank you, I guess. And speaking of things I need to know, there's something else I wanted to ask you. But it's kind of a silly question.'

'No matter, what do you want to ask?'

'Okay. Do you think there is any meaning to it all?' August asked pensively.

Rickard could sense the troubled man was grasping at straws, fighting to find reasons to justify his existence. He weighed his words greatly, wondering what would help August in this important moment. His intellect didn't provide any satisfying answers, so he let his nature speak freely.

'There's a grand birch in the park that greets me every morning.'

'What?'

'I think you heard me.'

August's head shook in confusion as a forceful frown raised itself between his brows.

'What the hell does that mean?'

'You'll see.'

'I don't think I will. I mean, you sound like a madman!' he retorted, giving off a nervous laugh. Rickard only replied with a smile.

'I ought to get some sleep, it's getting late. You should head home too, young man.'

'Yes, good idea. I don't know if I'll see you again, but I hope so'

August reached his hands toward Rickard, and they shared a warm embrace. Around them fallen leaves searched for their settling place on the moist ground as the grass danced gently to the tune of the nightly wind. August wanted to stay there, in the fire of his affection, but fears of someone spotting them crept into his mind, causing him to pull away.

'Good night, Rickard.'

'Night.'

The gentle sky had swallowed up the little seaside town into its immense darkness when the two men parted ways. As they left each other, Rickard reminisced on what his own life was like just before buying the book he handed over to the young man. It was a dismal time. It was a time when it was troublesome to find any pertinent reason to get out of bed in the mornings, and the surroundings of the little apartment he had rented in Chelsea didn't help much. People had stopped checking in on him at this point in his life, and the friends he used to know were ghosts in the wind. It was a time of serious grappling with the big question that a life presents; not much was beckoning him onwards while a whole lot was pulling him toward the other side.

If there was a hint certainty he would see his daughter again, he would have taken leave there and then. Unfortunately, we are an ignorant bunch, and we still haven't got any idea what happens when one passes the threshold. The thought of not seeing the people you love once more is deadening—even more so if you have lost a child. There is no greater loss in this world. It's unnatural that children should go before their parents, but it happens, and the effects are always devastating.

One morning around this time of his life, he walked along a busy street in London when he bumped into a little wooden trolley, inconveniently placed on the sidewalk. A few books fell off, and being the polite man he was, he placed them back, although a little annoyed. Then he realized he stood before a charming little secondhand bookshop. He stepped inside due to a queer infatuation with these shops in his youth. There was something peculiar about the ambiance of bookshops, so many lives and ideas floating round the room. There is also a hint of one's childhood cellar scent in those properly old shops, with wooden panels and too many books stacked up against the walls.

He wasn't looking for anything specific, but his being was attracted to a little room one could access by walking all the way in the back of the shop. A little sign was fixed above the room reading *Oriental philosophy and spirituality*. Rickard had never been interested in the area, and so he felt at odds with the part of him that wanted to explore it. Hesitantly he stepped through the narrow doorway and started scanning the shelves for anything that stood out. As he ran his fingers along the spines of the books on the shelf, one of the books fell to the floor. It gave him a scare, and he jumped back a little, then his eyes fell to the ground. The book landed cover down and he reached to grab the frail book. He had never heard of the title, and the cover art was unimpressive. Despite the unassuming façade, there was something alluring about the book.

'It wants to go home with you,' rang out from behind Rickard.

He swiftly turned around to find an old and tiny lady with semicircular glasses resting on her sharp nose.

'Haha, yes, you might be right—it jumped at me!'

'Yes, that happens on rare occasions. You'd be a fool not to listen. Tell me, what are you holding there?'

'It's called the *Tao Te Ching*. Do you know it?'

Why, of course I do, don't you?'

'No, never heard of it.'

'I have a feeling you'll come to know it quite well,' she said, giving off a murmuring laugh.

Then the entrance door was heard opening, and she fled towards it. He looked down at the book resting in his hand. The lady's comments, coupled with the inherent strange sensation he had felt about the book, stirred an unruliness in his being. He was curious to read the book now and started flipping through the pages slowly. Eager to learn about the strange book, he sought out the shopkeeper.

'Can you tell me a little more about the book? Who's the author, for example?'

'The man who wrote that is in the cross-section between myth and man, much like Christ in the West. His name was Lao-Tzu, and the legend goes that he was stopped by a curious customs agent as he was taking leave of his country. He convinced him to pass down some of his teaching before leaving for good, which resulted in a text consisting of eighty-one sayings. That text is considered the foundational text of Taoism, one of the two primary branches of philosophy in China.'

13

The murder investigation was launched at the turn of July and August. The young man quickly became a primary suspect to the police and had to return to the local station for several *interviews*, as they pleasantly called them, and by mid-September he was arrested on suspicion of murdering Mathias Hansen.

When Mathias's lifeless body first washed up on the beach, many believed it must have been a drunken accident that led to his death. Maybe a suicide even. All of that doubt was shredded when the pathologist considered the cause of death by blunt force trauma. From thereon, the real hunt for the murderer began in the otherwise peaceful town of Drøbak. The police ramped up the investigation, making it a national concern, but there wasn't much to go on. The only facts they had were that August had been the last to see Mathias and the cause of death. There wasn't anything out of the ordinary in Mathias' life, apart from the suspicion of abuse. From this, the police deduced that the young victim must have been exposed to an unfortunate episode of indiscriminate violence, or else

August was involved somehow. The suspicion of his involvement was strengthened by their love triangle, which could have caused bitterness and resentment in the young man.

The distress built each time August was brought in for questioning. Despite the difficulty, he maintained his equanimity with the help of Rickard's dreary vision of his future. Both Rickard and August thought the police would be forced to drop the case due to lack of any real evidence. That turned out to be poor judgment by the two men, as is often the case in a world like ours where politics prevails over facts.

In the month leading up to the arrest, August attended school as per usual, but life was different. People avoided speaking to him, his friends distanced themselves, and he felt isolated and persecuted. It became widely known that he had been the last person to see Mathias. The reason for the murder, the teenagers concluded, was rageful jealousy, as his former best friend had stolen his girlfriend. On the face of it, it was a thin motive, but it stuck like grease to an old pan, and the public opinion of their little town seemed to narrow in on this explanation too.

Throughout this, August continually pleaded his innocence, both to the police and generally, whenever a person was willing to hear him out. Even August's parents, as he had solemnly noticed, had had a change of character. They became less convinced of their own assertions of his innocence.

There had been funeral and a public memorial service for Mathias a few weeks after his body was discovered. August had been asked by his mother, who had spoken to Mathias' parents, not to attend the funeral out of respect for the family. He felt ashamed and neglected showing up to the memorial service as well, knowing how awful the whole scene would have felt.

The public condemnation made each day feel like a step closer to the gallows. Looks of scorn and fear were thrown at him wherever he ventured. He began dreading school, which he expressed to his parents, hoping to be able to convince them to let him do the last year of school at home. Sadly, they didn't buy into the idea and assured him that the difficult times would pass soon. Each day would be better than the next, his father kept telling him.

Ironically, the opposite was true, as each day brought increasing sorrow to the young man. As the school year began, he would eat his lunch in the canteen, sitting down by himself, hoping someone would join him. None ever did. All he was afforded were the hostile glances thrown at him. High school is a difficult phase as it is, but for August it was exponentially worse. All alone, surrounded by insecure teenagers, circled around tables, mumbling about the murderer allowed to walk their halls. He quickly sought other places to eat. He also started bringing food from home to avoid standing in the queue at the canteen. His grades began faltering, although he didn't feel like they should have—if anything, he was spending more time doing school now than ever, trying to distract himself with something worthwhile. But that's human beings, clearly unable to look at anything objectively. The prejudice given by the teachers enraged August, yet he was equally bothered by the same treatment from other students and inhabitants of their little town.

When the police inevitably came knocking on his door to take him away, he felt strangely joyous; finally, he would get out of that dreadful routine he had been trapped in. Despite this, he didn't plead guilty to anything. He wanted to hold himself to the promise he made on top of the mountain.

It is difficult to have one's freedoms taken away, no matter the age. However, for this to happen the same year real freedom has been granted is a pain difficult to describe. It's much like life never really began, he had been given a promise of a real life, yet when he arrived at the door, he was ushered away. Life for August had all but lost its thrust and grown stale.

From day one, he felt it was claustrophobic to be imprisoned. That horrid feeling didn't dwindle, only growing stronger over time, and became a constant property of his sad life. The only alleviating activity he would indulge in was when he let his mind wander and fantasize about how he could get out of there. Delusions of escape played tricks on him, yet actually getting out seemed impossible, as it should. And even if he, by some miracle, got out of those confines, where would he go? How far would he get if he got out? And when they inevitably caught up with him, he would be charged with attempted escape too. No, it was no great idea, although he found powerful romantic notions tied up with this idea of escape and living on the run. He would fantasize about this life; how he would change, live dangerously and all the people and places he would see. 'Silly infantile dreams,' he told himself, knowing full well there was no life in that. 'Oh, how I would do things differently if only…' he cried out in the night. The true sweetness of freedom cannot be grasped till it is violently taken away. Not encroached on little by little. No, there is no vitality or realization in that—only utter catastrophe will do the trick.

Weeks went by, and August started to grow anxious about his upcoming trial. His lawyer, whom his parents had hired, told them the chances of acquittal were reasonable; the police didn't appear to have much material evidence pointing obviously at August.

'It comes down to a sympathetic and reasonable jury. In my opinion, there is a real possibility you'll walk,' she had said.

His parents visited him twice a week, on Wednesdays and Saturdays at noon. They would get to spend forty-five minutes in a little room outfitted with two chairs, a dirty red rug, a couch, and a thirty-two-inch TV. When they first visited August, they would go on about the hopelessness and stupidity of the situation, as everyone knew full well he wouldn't hurt a soul. He would sit there, relatively quiet, and listen to their lament and preaching, but over time there was less and less talk. Increasingly the forty-five minutes were taken up by silence, instead of talking. August felt his parents were growing tired and unsure of the situation. It was a painful silence for all parties; no one knew what to say anymore. August started dreading their weekly meetings to the point of calling in sick numerous times when they stopped by. August's life was one of increasing isolation and despair; the only thing that kept his spirits alive was his avid clinging onto the words of hope: 'I might get out of this after all.'

14

Living day in and day out, as Rickard did, caused a healthy amount of loneliness. Mankind is a social being, and a life of relative solitude can be difficult at times, no matter how deeply or broadly one knows oneself. A significant upside, however, is the richness with which the inner life can well forth in an externally poor life. Tremendous joy and little grief are to be found there, but there's no lack of social and psychological costs.

Before he had settled in Drøbak, he wandered the streets of London for a few years. Life was enjoyable there, he had thought, but his heart longed for calm, a place with fewer people and richer nature. He wanted to be closer to the source of life. Namely, water, the ocean, and potential. Not some lousy polluted river running through an urban jungle. He scraped together the money for a plane ticket to Oslo and didn't look back.

He had spent time in Norway as a boy and had many pleasant memories from there. Teresa, his mother, was a Norwegian, and she had grown up on a farm there in the middle of that wretched poor country at the time. But riches didn't matter. They both held dearly that Norway encapsulated paradisal nature if nothing else.

Initially, when he first got back to Norway, he was an older man and established a little life; some social housing was eventually provided, he gained new friends, and he met a younger woman. Things looked bright, and Rickard felt satisfied. Yet that farce didn't last long, as he began growing tired, once again, of his rich external life at the expense of his inner life. These feelings contaminated his life in a number of ways: firstly, the woman lost interest in him, partly due to his impotence, and secondly, he gave up his housing. Her leaving didn't surprise him one bit; the only shock was that she took several months to get out of his life. He was grateful for having felt desired, perhaps truly for the last time, by the fairer sex. As for the housing, he kept fantasizing about living outside, instead of being trapped in an artificially heated box.

This desire derived, partly, from the need to be free. Free from the help of others, control, but beyond all of that, true freedom from any material need and the many fetters it brings. He fondly remembered the tranquil peace he had experienced living on the streets in a small village outside of London for a few weeks. This was a feeling he had lost since he travelled north. This culminated in Rickard discovering a law, which he named the *law of simplicity*: the level of voluntary simplicity in your life corresponds directly to your degree of harmony.

About fifty meters from the city square, there was a little kiosk that Rickard would visit sometimes in the mornings during the weekdays. A teenage girl was working there, Julie, who kindly let him fill a cup of hot water for free at their coffee machine. She only worked a few days of the week, from 7:30 to 13:00, which happened to be the only time Rickard visited the kiosk.

Earlier that year, he was walking through the city as usual when he glanced through the pane of the kiosk. On the other side, he met an unusually kind gaze from a young girl. She smiled politely at him, then turned away. That moment filled old Rickard with joy, and the following day he went into the kiosk to introduce himself. At first, he hesitated, as he was afraid she might feel horrified about an old bum speaking to her. Yet the need for social contact was overpowering, so he went ahead despite his reservations. Sure enough, she was a sweet soul, and they exchanged a few pleasantries: names and such. He wished her a lovely day, and as he was walking out, she said, 'Let me know if there's anything I can do to help out.'

She didn't need to do that. Nobody told her to say that; it came from the purity of her heart. Over the next week, Rickard brooded over what she might do for him. At first, he wanted nothing — he was overjoyed she had shown him any compassion. Then, he remembered how much he enjoyed having a cup of coffee during his younger days. It had been several months, if not years, since last he had some. There was only tea at Martha's place too, which made coffee difficult to consume. There and then, he decided to buy a jar of instant coffee, as he felt certain the sweet girl would be happy to offer some hot water. Then, when the months turned cold, he could bring it to Martha's place.

'How did I not think of this before?' he wondered humorously.

He rummaged around in his suitcase to locate his paper cup with a plastic top lid. Next, he got his half-empty instant coffee jar, opened it, then poured a little into the cup. He preferred the coffee to be weak, probably since he had never been an avid drinker. He closed up the suitcase, covered it as usual, and placed the plastic lid in his blazer pocket. He emerged out of the bushes and headed toward the kiosk with the cup in hand. On the way, he walked past an old couple, walking hand in hand, throwing deadly eyes at the ragged man.

'Good morning,' he said but received no response. *Imbeciles, the whole lot of them!* he screamed inside his head, feeling the growing suspicion by inhabitants to be revolting.

Outsiders are easy to blame and ostracize; it happens time and time again, in different guises—this was another version of that. *Thank god everyone isn't that shallow*, he thought as he entered the kiosk. Another man was at the checkout counter, buying a hotdog with an array of add-ons. Julie noticed him as he entered. Normally, she would have given a slight smile and nodded toward the coffee machine. This time, however, fear filled her innocent gaze. Rickard was ashamed as he realized that she, like most people, imagined he was behind the murder. He felt stupid and like getting out of there but figured he would fill his cup before leaving. 'This will be my last cup of water from here,' he resolved. He filled the cup to the brim, took a small wooden stick, and mixed the powder around, then he headed straight for the door. Before he exited, he looked over at her despondently.

'Don't worry, dear, I won't be back.'

With his steaming cup of coffee and a gloomy cloud above him, he moved about the streets of Drøbak. At first, he walked over to the old cinema, lying a hundred paces from the kiosk. Two movie posters were plastered on each side of the entry door, one for a cartoon movie called Jimmy's Grand Jungle Adventure and the other for a traditional film titled Out of the Euphrates. It had been decades since Rickard had seen a film in the movie theater. 'Maybe I'll go one of these days,' he told himself as he continued strolling down the street. On the opposite side of the cinema, there was a barber shop and, next to it, a joint clothing and jewelry store, both boutiques run by local women. Rickard hadn't been inside either of them, but he enjoyed looking through the windows of the shops, seeing the people chatting and walking about.

It was a rather narrow street with tall wooden houses that stretched for a hundred and fifty meters from the city square, after which the street diverged and you'd enter a residential area. This street, called Storgata, was mostly made up of restaurants and shops, with the odd residential apartment on top of the buildings. Everything was painted white and red, and broad sidewalks were placed on the sides of the street, with a narrowly paved asphalt road in the middle. It was humorously narrow, nearly causing trouble every time two cars met.

The streets were empty now; people at work, school, or rotting away in some home, be it their own or a nursery. The weather was dull, and Rickard was in a corresponding mood, however, the coffee perked up his mood a little. At the end of the street, he had taken a right toward the water, where he could follow another path that circled back toward the city center and the local harbor. The wind was blowing that morning, so drops of seawater kissed his face as he moved along the ocean on a narrow flower-ridden path.

'What a treat to be alive!' he said out loud, as he walked past a statue of a mermaid, placed at the foot of the sea, overlooking the simmering waters and the land on the opposite side of the fjord. It had been created by some inspired Norwegian artist a hundred years back, apparently symbolizing some legend called Atargatis, which would not be obvious had it not been carved into the stone below the little creature.

It's curious that there are so many legends of mermaids. Maybe there was a time when they roamed the oceans—perhaps they still do—but have learned to be stealthy, only appearing at night before home-sick and sexually frustrated seamen. Rickard hummed thinking about it.

He continued walking along the little gravel path hugging the coastline till he spotted a familiar face. An older lady was sitting on a bench, her hair blowing in all directions, with a book in hand and her cane placed neatly across her lap. Rickard approached her smilingly.

'What brings you to the sea, young woman?'

She was a little startled at first, then overtaken with happiness to be greeted by her friend.

'Ah, good to see you again! Come, come, take a seat. Isn't it magnificent,' she said, scanning the view before them. 'I brought a little literature, but I never end up reading.'

'Understandable, there's nothing more poetic than nature herself,' he said.

They sat in silence, gazing at the winding wind manipulating the surface of the water; the dance of nature fills the soul with sublime light when given the chance.

'It's an utter tragedy, the death of that young man. And to think something like that could happen here? In our peaceful little town, I don't understand it.'

Rickard nodded in agreement.

'My grandchild goes to the same high school as that poor boy did! And also, the one that's been arrested!' she said, looking worriedly over at him.

Rickard was startled. 'Arrested?' he blurted out.

'Yes, apparently they're holding a boy on suspicion of murder. August, I think his name was.' Martha took notice of Rickard's uneasiness, wondering why he was reacting so strongly.

'What's the matter, Rickard?'

His head was flooded with unpleasant questions; did they have something on him? Would August tell them how the body was moved? Am I next? He started sweating slightly and sat there antsy, trying desperately to find his words.

'Oh, I'm just thinking about that kid, the one that's been arrested,' he answered at last, surmising it would be beneficial to tell some of the truth, at the very least.

'He's a kind kid with a big heart. You probably didn't know, but he is essentially the only person in this town that speaks to me. Well, aside from you. I saw a boy went missing in the newspapers a while back. Then August comes along, more anxious than I had ever seen him, and goes on to tell me he had been the last person that poor boy saw before he disappeared. Yes, talk about bad luck! I can't imagine he had anything to do with the murder.'

She looked at him curiously. 'I understand, of course; I'm sure the poor boy is innocent. But the whole thing does sound a little suspicious, don't you think?'

Rickard didn't know what to say, feeling an impending doom about to strike him down. 'I have to get out of this town' he told himself, as he sat there looking down at his lazy feet.

'Cheer up, Rickard! I'm certain the boy didn't do anything, if he is as kind as you are suggesting, I can't imagine he will be found guilty of such a horrendous act,' she said with a compassionate smile, Plus, my grandchild told me he's telling the police, and anyone that will listen, that he is innocent!'

Rickard barely heard what she said, thinking only about where to go from here. He needed to get out of there; the last thing he wanted to do was spend the last years of his life rotting away in some cell. He needed to get out of Drøbak, out of Norway, and settle someplace far away, quietly. He couldn't stand sitting there, nor remain in the city a second longer than necessary, in fear of August revealing the truth. He gulped down the rest of his coffee, excused himself as innocuously as he could muster, and then started running toward Lincoln as soon as he was out of Martha's sight.

He gathered all his essential belongings in his suitcase, including his clothes, pillow, sleeping bag, and a large bottle of water. The green tarp he had used to wrap the bench and his belongings he discarded due to lack of space. He grabbed his heavy suitcase and strolled laboriously over to the square, where there was a bus stop.

He jumped on the next bus to Oslo, figuring he would sketch out a plan on the way into the capital. He had to wait about fifteen minutes before the bus arrived, and it was nearly empty. There was an older lady with a hat sitting up front, whilst a fat man with a headset was blasting rock music at the back. Rickard took a seat in the middle of the bus, right before the doors, as it was easiest to store the suitcase there.

As he moved further out of that wretched little town, a sense of relief consumed the old man. He hoped August could keep his innocence and leave his involvement out of the picture. As he couldn't know what he would do, he felt he was doing the only rational thing there was to do. One must look after one's own interest in this world.

He pondered where it made sense to travel and how to get there. Looking out the bus window as they approached Oslo, he glimpsed a cruise. The large boat was gliding gracefully through the water, heading toward the harbor of Oslo. It reminded him of the Danish ferry, as it's called in Norway, that carried people between Oslo and Copenhagen.

'That's it,' he concluded cheerfully. Tickets to travel to Denmark by boat were cheap. While traveling he would have plenty of time to think about what to do next, and he could spend a comfortable night in a cabin. Getting out into the ocean also appealed to the old man, who hadn't been out there for decades, despite loving the calmness it brings.

15

The spring was shuffling into its later stages as Rickard and August walked among coy and merry trees in the local park, engaged in lively conversation.

'I spent many nights, late at bars, chasing the eyes of beautiful women. Then, from catching their feline gaze, I'd attempt to lure them in and bring them home. That's harder than it sounds, at least for a man like me, anyway. My appearance is not very agreeable. Put bluntly, I'm an ugly bastard. Still, I succeeded enough times to realize the utter blind road that way of life was! I thought all I wanted was to feel desired and longed after, but that's a spectacularly hollow pursuit; let me be the first to tell you. No, I've found that it's preferable to find one mate, a person you feel excited about sharing life with. All we're certain of is this life, so isn't it logical that you want to find another person to love and explore deeply? Life is short, and jumping from flower to flower will provide plenty of pollen, but you won't experience the grace that is true love and devotion.

'My ex-wife, bless her and her delicate soul—oh, how thankful I am to have met her. I didn't get to spend my whole life with her, but the years we shared were a lifetime's worth. Yes, it's a true gift to meet the person you're supposed to. The one made specifically for you — that's how it should feel, anyway. I'd give my life for another moment with my two angels together.'

'Two? Who is the second then?' asked August.

'My daughter, I'll tell you a little about her in a moment, if I must, but there's something else I need to get off my chest. At some point in your life, you're bound to think this, as I surely did: You become convinced that you want to be alone. I need to be alone. To ponder, to think deeply about this and that. Then you drink, and instantly you're longing for a companion once again. Like an onrush of insight that you were scared to admit to. It's a woman you want before you, one you can play with and sway. Ah, how despicable we are. That's just the shallow nature of man I suppose. But we may also penetrate that layer of desire and find something else! Something better, something more real. Sadly, it appears impossible unless one leaps into the divine, which has been hollowed out in modern times.

'I'm not so sure I will think that at all. I really enjoy hanging out with people. Especially my friends. Some of the best memories I have are with friends: late nights, drinking, and having a blast.'

Rickard smiled at August, like one smiles at a beautifully naive child.

'I like to think of alcohol as a *faux amis*—do you know the expression? No? Well, it's a French grammatical term, but no matter. The way I see it is that a drink will make you feel joyous and glad, but it doesn't have your best interest in mind. In other words, it's a friend who's fun to hang with but cannot be trusted.

'I had one of those once, a *faux amis*, except this one was encapsulated by flesh and blood and not a glass bottle. Of course, I thought of him as a great friend, up until a moment; if only we were able to tell these things in advance. Let me tell you a little about him; it might be a good thing for you to know.

'At some point in my life, I wanted to set up a little business: a newspaper booth that would sell papers, books, snacks, and things of that nature. Now it probably sounds crazy, but decades ago, back in London, this was a wonderful business model! I had to scrape together some capital to get the thing started, and George was the only guy I convinced, the only one willing to take a chance on me. Thanks to him I got my stand started, and in less than six months I was turning a handsome profit. It was incredible and I shared the happy news with George; I can still picture his proud face before me.

'Months later he happened upon my little stand, looking awfully worked up and terrified. He told me all about some legal troubles he was in. About how it was draining his resources and destroying his family life. He needed money soon, otherwise, the nail in his coffin was rapidly approaching; his business and marriage would be placed several feet under the ground, never to be exhumed. I felt sorry for the old chap, and so I helped him out. My new business meant I was able to take out a loan, which I happily handed over to George. He kissed my face and hands when I turned up at his place with the check and legal papers. He promised to have it all back within half a year, which sounded perfectly fine by me.

'We agreed he would provide weekly updates, which he did for a while. But those weekly calls turned into biweekly updates, and finally all communication fell through the floor. Suddenly, I couldn't get hold of him. That's when the panic started creeping in. Surely, he would get back soon, I tried assuring myself. At a certain point, I reached out to his wife due to my mounting anxieties. She told me George had left the country over two weeks ago without a word. She was happy to be rid of her deadbeat husband and hoped she'd never see him again. During that conversation, the weight of the mighty world felt heavier on my weak shoulders than ever before. I never saw the money, nor that greedy fellow again. Ironically, the man who helped start my little business also managed to close it down. All that to say, I prefer one *faux amis* to the other.

'Friendships have been rare and far between ever since I reached my forties. Even good friends I used to have abandoned me. In some ways I understand it; I was an insufferable prick, and it must have taken a miracle to enjoy my company. Then again, the way I acted wasn't exactly out of line, considering what'd happened. Ah, the bloody mess that was my life back then.'

'You mentioned your daughter earlier; is she somehow connected to this *bloody mess* you're talking about? Do you still have a relationship with her?'

'Sadly, no. We lost her at a young age, our poor little girl. There's no greater evil, if such a thing exists, than the loss of your precious child. It was devastating for Juliet and me. I fell apart. Nobody was there to pick up the pieces, least of all myself, and so my life became an untended garden with ugly weeds growing all over. Some intangible, yet real and important, part of me died with her; joy lost its sweetness, love stopped reaching old heights, and melancholy became my drug of choice.'

'I'm so sorry, Rickard.'

'It's many years ago now. I'm an old man and there's little that gives rise to real hurt anymore, Astrid being the only exception. I still think about her every day.'

Rickard lowered his head and began rubbing his temples between his left thumb and index finger. An image of her appeared in the eye of his mind. Her tender eyes would be the answer he would serve if God himself asked for the meaning of life; you'll find it all there, the animating spirit of love abides in the gaze of our children. There's nothing greater to experience in this world. Sure, it comes with a myriad of worries, but that's a small price to pay. If given one wish it would be to give his dear child another chance at the life she was forsaken. Rickard was woeful that the world was deprived of the opportunity to see her heart unfold itself in many beautiful ways.

'I'd like to have a family one day,' the young man said.

'Good. I'm glad to hear it, August.'

'Look, I better get going. It's been lovely seeing you as always, Rickard. I'll swing by again later this week; hopefully, you'll be here. I'm so excited for the good weather to come back now. Summer is right around the corner again!' he exclaimed with a grin.

16

Rickard stepped off the bus at the capital's central station, thinking he would walk around town a little before going to where the ferry departed. He arrived at the city just past noon, which meant the cruise wouldn't leave for Denmark for another six hours. It was a pleasant day; clear skies and the warmth rubbed up against the timid old man. Normally, a blessed day like this would generate joy in him, but Rickard's mind was uneasy. He had just learned August had been incarcerated, causing tremendous grief in the old man. He had done all he could to rid him of the burden that is prison. He knew that the egregious deed he had committed would be punishment enough for the young man—landing in prison would neither be helpful nor necessary. All of that was useless speculation now unless he was able to exonerate himself somehow.

Rickard's head was lowered in deep thought as he wandered along Karl Johan. The streets were thin and filled by university students and retired people walking about aimlessly. Rickard, almost without realizing it, steered off the street and into a nearby park. Having walked between the trees and grass for a while, he looked up and left his thoughts wandering by themselves. His arms went behind his back, hand in palm, and he walked slowly, observing the hidden wildlife simmering around, only noticeable when given a little attention. Birds were playing on branches, flying back and forth, laughing amongst each other. A little squirrel was also out for a stroll, much like him, yet the rascal was a little more adventurous than him, exploring the end of a thin branch, high in the air. He slumped down on the grass, absorbed by the sight of the pretty rat with the brown coat. Through the branches of the trees, one saw glimmers of small clouds and the sun penetrating through the few empty spaces. He reveled in the gracious manner the little creature was moving about the scattered branches.

'Splendid nature and spontaneity,' he murmured, digging his hands, which were planted slightly behind him, into the moist soil.

He spent considerable time in that park, surrounded by the odd jogger and the lively nature. He lingered on what his life would look like months from now: Where will I be, and what will I be doing? Perhaps he could travel further down south in Europe, reaching someplace where he could spend all year outside. That would make life a little easier, not having to depend on anyone. Being fully immersed in nature without constraints. This serene image finally poured some gladness into the old man's heart. He dreamt about bushes bringing forth berries and fruit trees that would sustain him. Maybe even a small patch of dirt that he could cultivate?

Finally, he strolled over to one of the exits of the park. On the right-hand side there stood a queer tree: an old, fat and gnarled oak tree with wicked branches spread about. Calling it strange would be an understatement, and it brought a boyish smile to Rickard's face. He stood there savoring its majestic nature for a while, then he walked through the gates. He was immediately greeted by a tall grey building. It was dull and reached fifty meters into the skies. It was unimaginative and functional, likely serving as an office building.

'There we have it,' he said, 'the specter of mankind.'

A grievous sensation occupied his bosom as he stood before that grey manmade box. All societal norms and expectations function as a great factory press, making those grey-boxed humans with a higher degree of dull perfection every year. If only the pendulum would swing back occasionally. No matter, he thought, all I control is my own life. Let's not lose sight that all change begins locally.

God, how Rickard longed to be that dancing tree instead of the stone square; the former is creativity, life even, in the truest sense of the word, while the latter is sterility and death.

While the old fellow contemplated these things, he made his way over to the docks, where the boat would depart. He made it to the water and walked alongside the rowdy dock all the way there. Eventually, he spotted the cruise quayside, a few hundred meters up ahead. He found a lonesome bench and retired there for a while, enjoying the view of the Oslo Fjord one last time.

Apart from the cruise ship he was about to board, there were a handful of sailboats sliding through the rough waters. There was also a feeder ship heading to the commercial harbor, presumably carrying garments, shoes, or so. The water was moving wildly about due to a fresh breeze coming over the northeastern valley. Rickard stared out at the blue with a contorted smile.

His head began shaking slightly and he looked down at the funny tremble.

'What am I doing?'

One was almost able to make out Drøbak from where he sat. Rickard felt small in that moment, sitting there by his lonesome. The weight of his selfish cowardice was oppressing; he couldn't very well leave that young man alone. The only man that had shown him his heart. The only man that had shown him there was brotherly love in this world. Almost everyone else turned their cold shoulder to him, and his suffering didn't influence them one bit. No, he deserved more. August deserved a life! That which was being taken away from him at this very moment.

It also dawned on him that Martha had mentioned he had maintained his innocence throughout this. If that was still the case, he figured, then there was a chance; he could take his place. As the thought registered, a splendid calm consumed the old man. The tension that had been brooding since the talk with Martha early that morning loosened its grip, finger by finger.

Rickard saw this self-sacrifice as a step toward a more harmonious world. In August, he saw a loving young man with his life before him; he has the opportunity to enjoy and contribute so much to this life, spread across all the years he has left. Rickard's life was already approaching the sunset, an experience we will all be privy to. No, he didn't need much. To know he had helped someone he loved would be more than sufficient. Prison would provide excessive comforts for him so he could get by easily. To live out the rest of his life in some warm environment, playing bridge, tuckering away in some workshop, and at peace with himself—yes, that wouldn't be all that bad.

17

Rickard decided to give up his life for August. But before hanging his proverbial coat up indefinitely, it was only logical to burn his emergency fund. A hundred paces from the city square there was a shoddy bar named *The Shoe*. You'll find it by traversing a narrow path squeezed between two buildings on the boulevard running through the city. This place is hidden from plain sight, as it is mostly reserved for degenerates; alcoholics and people with a *significant* string of bad luck. The kind of people who prefer not being seen walking in and out of a bar. It's charming, really, in a gross manner, with its dim lighting and cigarette smoke swimming above the sticky wooden floor panels. The old man had been there once before, but he didn't buy anything then, as he felt he couldn't afford it. Also, he was a cheap man, hating to waste the little money he possessed. But he remained curious about the place, as he had seen numerous drunks stumbling in and out of that narrow passageway. This time, however, his motivation for going was different. This time, he was stepping into the place a *wealthy* man;

fifteen hundred neatly folded kroner burned in his pocket.

It was late afternoon when he arrived back at Drøbak. He stepped off at the city square and went by the supermarket to pick up a card and an envelope. He borrowed a pen from the cashier, rested the card on a wall, and wrote:

Dear Martha,

You're about to discover a terrible thing I've done. For that, I'm truly sorry. Thank you from the bottom of my soul for all the kindness and generosity you've shown me since I arrived here, all those years ago. You truly are one of the best people I've met. My remaining years will be spent atoning for my sins and reading great literature—did you ever read the story of King Lycurgus? Anyhow, I wish you several beautiful years before reuniting with your beloved husband.

Yours truly,

Rickard

He placed the card in the envelope, sealed it, and wrote *Martha* on the front. Then he strolled over to her house. Approaching her gate, he could see her walking about in the living room. He considered seeing her one last time. To hand her the letter and tell her to open it the next day. But that would have been foolish, and he felt ashamed to face her, so he slid the letter into her mailbox and savored a last gaze at her and her abode before walking off. He found it difficult to part with her this way. He knew she would hold him in disdain till the day she passed; there was little doubt in his heart, and it caused a lavish pain in Rickard. He cared for her and her kind heart, and this was how she would remember him. Despite this, he knew there were things in life more important than relationships and how someone views you, regardless of your compassion for them—the important thing is to walk the path as it reveals itself.

From her house he walked back toward the city square, taking a right on the boulevard. The narrow path appeared on his right, and he slipped in. It was dark, and the ground was covered by moist bridge stone and moss. Twelve paces from the street, one arrived before a wooden door with a sign holstered above. It read *The Shoe* and there was a sad illustration of worn-out footwear beside it. He walked through the creaky door, and a small and dimly lit place was revealed. There were two tables to his right and one to his left, with a bar counter in line with the door. It was a dark and dirty slab of wood and steel with four bar stools placed before it. Behind the counter stood a fat old lady with a black apron. Her sly eyes centered on him as he opened the door. He was all alone, which he savored.

'Good day, what can I get you?' she said with a gruff voice, the type of voice only producible by a hard life accompanied by the consumption of too many cigarettes.

'A pint of draft beer, please,' he replied.

He scanned the liquor bottles on display behind her. An unimpressive collection of bottles stood on a thin shelf behind the lady: a bottle of absolute vodka, a half-finished Jameson whiskey and some Havana rum. A moment after scanning the depressive spirits selection, a beer, foaming slightly off the edge of the glass, was placed before him.

'Ring the bell if you'd like another,' she said with her gaze oddly hovering above him. Then she slipped into a room behind the bar counter, busying herself with something. He rang that bell many times, as he sat there alone, contemplating his decision.

A bed, food, and community; prison doesn't sound all that bad. Above all of that, he would give a young man the gift of life back. This idea of his life amounting to at least one good deed felt valuable to the decrepit and now drunken man. He snapped out of his train of thought when the door slid open behind him. A slight breeze kissed his neck, and he turned around. A middle-aged man with a melancholic look wandered in, wrapped in a thin black trench coat. Rickard gave a slight nod to welcome the stranger, who returned the gesture and sat down on the far end of Rickard's right side. The woman crept out from the back again.

'What will it be?'

'A double shot of whiskey,' he replied with a monotone voice.

'I'll have one more too, thank you,' the old man chimed in, pointing to his half-empty glass. The two men sat there drinking in silence, protected from the oppressive reality resting outside the thin wooden paneled walls, enjoying each other's mute company.

'Do you believe in evil?' the stranger suddenly asked, looking down at his shot glass, swirling the contents gently around. The old man glanced over at him, noting the hollow look in his eyes. Rickard was compelled to guess what brought him through those doors. Perhaps he was fired? Maybe he discovered his wife had strayed?

Yes, probably infidelity, he thought, as the man sat fiddling with his wedding ring.

'I don't.'

The man looked up at him in surprise.

'Really? How's that?'

'Well, I'm not so sure there is such a thing as good or evil; they simply are. It's only our limited view that places a layer of value judgment upon the world.'

The man shook his head in disbelief.

'So, you don't think rape or the damn Holocaust can be considered evil?'

'I guess I don't, no.'

He was clearly perplexed by the novel answer, unsure how to go from there. Can someone say something that disqualifies further conversation? Probably, yes, but wouldn't one want to dive deeper into the mind of such a strange creature? Suddenly the stranger's disgusted face turned into one of relief. The man downed the rest of his shot, then continued, 'I am leaving my wife and children next week.'

'Aha.'

'I feel like a real bastard, you know. But I'm going after the life I've always wanted.' He paused for a moment, tilting his head slightly up as a twisted smile formed.

'There's this gorgeous young girl I met last year; Natasha's her name. We're moving to Lisbon together; I've already rented a great apartment. When I get there I'll drink, fuck, eat and simply pursue all my lascivious desires like a dog. God, how great it'll be! And best of all she's open-minded, you know; she doesn't care that I chase tail. That's my Shangri-La. Since I don't know what's waiting for me on the other side, I'm determined to make the best of what I've got here and now, I'll build my paradise right here on earth.'

He looked down at his shot glass once more. 'But I can't help but feel evil and guilty for leaving them behind.'

Rickard listened with eagerness, sipping his beer occasionally. The man's monologue had ended, and he looked depleted and further away from paradise than most.

'Perhaps there is evil after all,' he said with a smile.

The man didn't appreciate the joke, and he turned his body away, feeling hurt. 'Have you done anything I'd consider evil then?' he finally threw back.

'Sure, I've had a long life,' Rickard replied.

'That's vague. Anything you'd like to get off your chest? I'd like to hear it; perhaps I'll feel better about myself.'

'I have many sins to atone for, in fact, the last chapter of my life will be devoted to just that,' he said with a tranquil look on his face.

'No kidding, I can tell by the look of you. There's no doubt you did some downright reprehensible things. Isn't that right?'

He didn't reply. He sat there indifferently, which had the effect of further infuriating the trench-coated man. He reached for his glass once more, finished the last bit, then placed the last bit of his emergency fund before him. When the money hit the sticky wood, the old witch came rushing out from the back. Apparently, she had learned to recognize the sound of valuable paper hitting the counter. Rickard looked over at the dark-featured man, then said, 'What you're envisioning as paradise is the paradise of an infantile adolescent, not a grown man. Soon enough, those free frames you'll have created will turn empty, shallow, and hellish. Think twice about what to do. Trust me, I've seen it before.' He patted the man's shoulder, then left the joint and walked onto the boulevard.

The sunlight bathed his face as the graceful combination of drunkenness and resolve simmered in his being. He turned his nose towards the local police station, which was located fifteen minutes by foot from the city center.

He opened the door to the station; there was no one there but an old and chubby man with spectacles, who sat behind a wooden counter. The man's droopy and large eyes rose from his newspaper when the door slammed open.

'What can I do you for?' he said with a jovial voice.

'I'd like to turn myself in for the murder of that teenage kid who washed up on the beach the other day. My name's Rickard Wilhelm.'

'Okay…' he said with a trembling voice, clearly disconcerted about being alone in the room with this self-proclaimed murderer. 'Just take a seat over there; I'll have someone over momentarily. You'll just need to wait a little, alright?'

'No, I won't,' he replied with a stern voice, causing the poor man to jump up from his seat in petrifaction. He had no idea how to respond to this crazy old man and probably feared him throwing himself toward him across his desk, which suddenly felt awfully small.

'I'm only joking, I'll be right here,' Rickard said moments later, after leading the fellow on for a while too long.

Rickard was picked up, questioned, and then placed in a prison on the outskirts of Oslo to await his trial. His cell was a neat little room, with a small desk, a single bed, and a separate bathroom. Ironically, he lived under significantly better conditions now than he had in years. Despite this, he missed living outside. He longed for the splendor of nature.

There was a common area where prisoners could talk, play games, watch TV, and whatever else they could come up with, but he didn't spend much time there. Some of his fellow prisoners made him feel uneasy, and so he preferred to spend time in the workshop, library, and his bedroom. Every evening, he'd be lying down in his bed, which pleasantly displayed the sky through a window across from him. He missed the beauty and simplicity of his old life. Although he was locked up, he still participated in nature. Through his barred window he watched soft painted strokes of skies moving gently across the frame. Every evening, he sought refuge in the dusking sky; its explosive beauty was the closest thing to heaven he'd been able to find in this last chapter of his life.

18

Tears of joy were shed when August learned Rickard had admitted to the killing of Mathias. The police were terribly sorry about the anxiety and despair they had brought upon August and his family. The young man didn't care at all, although his parents felt they certainly deserved an apology. The joy of re-attaining his freedom overshadowed all the terrible things that had happened in the last few months.

He was picked up by his father at the police station who embraced his son like never before. He felt like he met an unknown man with a greater paternal love than he had ever known. A man who brimmed with gladness and relief. His old man went on cursing the wretched authorities for questioning his innocence, repeating this notion, the whole ride home. That said, it was a merry car ride for both, particularly for August who felt that profound elation only afforded people who stroll above the law. When he retired to bed that night he lay there for hours, feeling deeply grateful to Rickard. How could I ever repay him? He made several promises to God that night about how he would conduct his life from here on.

It would be a virtuous and compassionate life, he promised. It was only right. To bring justice to the chance given to him by that saintly bum and to honor Mathias' memory.

As August's life went back to *normal,* those promises were quickly forgotten, and there turned out to be little that resembled his old life. His popularity at school, which was negligible but not non-existent before Mathias' disappearance, sky-rocketed when he came back. Most students and teachers fixed their eyes on him as he walked past them in the halls of the school.

An unbridled confidence began rising in August, which everyone around him noticed—it generated an attraction and a charisma that people sought. Increasingly, he was invited to parties during the weekends. His friends began reusing the dead group chat that had been abandoned when Mathias' body was discovered. These days they fought for his attention, to an irritating degree sometimes, both in and outside of school. Girls also took a markedly higher interest in August. By now he was asked to go to cinemas and cafes weekly, something unheard of before. Unsurprisingly, it solidified and grew the young man's ego.

The experience was both overwhelming and intoxicating for August, who got exposed to two polar opposites of life over a short period. Everything changed between going to prison and returning to school. It was disconcerting to see how easily people changed their behavior and attitudes towards him, only based on arbitrary notions. Naturally, it wasn't completely arbitrary, as they had viewed him as a murderous perpetrator, but throughout all of that, he had claimed he was innocent. Innocent, for God's sake! That didn't matter; people usually believe the worst—it's where our minds travel with the least resistance. Us humans are extraordinarily judgmental, something August got to discover firsthand.

Despite this, he enjoyed the new attention he was awarded. He was excited about the newfound interest from the fairer sex and the many parties he was invited to every weekend, even receiving invites from strangers. They were people from cities nearby who had heard about the case and were intrigued by his story that had garnered some national attention. It's rather compelling to be the victim of a wrongful conviction that made its way into the newspapers. It all culminated in a fleeting moment of national fame for August when it was reported that he was innocent. It pleased both him and his friends that they are allowed to tag along to these parties. He savored the feeling of specialness. Being a celebrity must be quite the treat, he thought, as he wondered how he could solidify his image and ride this wave of popularity.

There was a sense of being untouchable. He was a head above the herd, and there was a fervor that propelled him toward adventure, which intoxicated the young man. He was filled with passion and virility, really sensing the world lying before his feet as if the world had been molded exactly for him to tread into, manipulate and savor. Maybe the stark contrast of his state of mind from recently made his experience even more intense. More than ever, he felt at ease with himself and the world. He also began to view the world differently; getting away with his transgression had shown him an avenue of action available to the strong-minded person. A possibility he didn't even imagine, but now he saw that the fate of one's life really lay in one's own hands. It was only weak-minded shackles that prevented one from gripping life by its collar and directing it as you see fit.

In school, he obtained better marks than before despite putting in less work, which made little sense to

August. He concluded it was the teachers trying to make up for the negative prejudice they had showered him with after Mathias' disappearance. On more than one occasion, his teacher asked for a word after class. Here they would express their deep empathy for how difficult it all must have been, being wrongfully blamed for the murder of a classmate and good friend. August pretended this was deeply touching to him, which the teachers gladly bought, only fueling their pity campaign.

These experiences reinforced a new notion August stumbled upon: mankind's utter inability to be objective.

Mathias' parents also came to visit his family house one evening. They arrived with deeply troubled faces, expressing their regret for the horrible way they had treated August, asking him not to attend Mathias' funeral, and believing he was responsible for their son's death. They pleaded his forgiveness while blaming their stupendous irrationality on the difficulties that go along with losing the dearest thing in the world. August was full of forgiveness, telling them he held nothing against them and that he understood. When they left, he could see the gleaming pride in his parents' eyes, which practically screamed, 'What a man we've raised!'

19

The days of late autumn were filled with elation and joy for August. He had put that difficult chapter of his life behind him, and although he felt sorry for Rickard, the feeling of gratitude and serenity was overpowering. He really felt it was all behind him now, people were no longer looking at him with suspicion, nor were they avoiding him. In fact, he was more social and thrived more than any other period in his life. Everyone was his friend, and he enjoyed the attention of most.

During the weekends he would frequent parties, often several during a night, as he and his friends were pulled and invited all over the place. A few months ago, he had hardly gone to any party outside a radius of 20 kilometers of Drøbak. Now, he was often traveling into the capital, enjoying house parties in extravagant houses and promiscuous girls. There had been national coverage of the murder case, so his name was widely known. People were quick to find August on Instagram and suddenly his popularity was soaring. He took great advantage of it too, garnering a few thousand followers. This only grew the willingness for people to move around his circles, simply to be associated him. Stefan Zweig spoke of the radiant power of fame, a certain essence that exerted a poignant effect on others; this wasn't far away from what August developed around this time.

A few friends were resting on a bench after meeting up to play some football at August's old elementary school one evening. He enjoyed coming back to this school sometimes. It was a place marked by good memories and thrilling times. Most have a nostalgic view of their youth, August being no exception. His heart was filled with a certain gladness every time they killed some time there.

'A girl, Cornelia Wallenberg, messaged me yesterday. Have you heard of her?' said August.

'No. But the last name's familiar. Is she one of the heirs of that industrialist?'

'Maybe. She looks stunning at least, and she invited us to a party tonight.'

'Ah, great,' exclaimed Alexander.

'Where is it?' asked another friend.

'It's some address in Holmenkollen,' August replied with a grin.

'God damn! It must be the daughter of that rich bastard.'

'Haha, yeah, it might be. Try looking up the address, it's called Esplanadenvei 12.'

Alexander fumbled his phone from his pocket and threw the address into the search engine. His eyes widened which caught the attention of the teenagers who sat around the table.

'What does it look like?'

'It's fucking massive. It looks like a mansion, or maybe a castle. Even the entrance of the place looks grand, like nothing I've seen, and there also seems to be a roundabout with a fountain before the entrance of the house. It's preposterous!'

'Perfect,' August said slyly. 'I'll tell her I look forward to seeing her.'

The group decided to take the bus to Oslo and split the cost of a cab from there to the party. Along the bus ride they humorously swapped stories and insults, consuming copious amounts of beer and poorly mixed cocktails from old plastic bottles. As they arrived in Oslo, their spirits were high, and the arousal continued all the way to the *chateau.*

The facade of the house was menacing, with four Ionic columns embracing the entrance door. At each end of the face, two towers with pointed roofs were seen, which made August think of Saint Petersburg. A few expensive cars were parked outside, neatly lined up on both sides of the staircase to the entrance.

'I wouldn't mind one of these for my birthday,' said Alexander with a tinge of sadness in his voice. The thought that this lifestyle was beyond any future in store for them was unyielding. It was a symbol of generational wealth that no one person could hope to garner in one lifetime, although there are naturally a handful of exceptions to the rule.

They were a group of five guys, including August, Alexander, Erik and two others. As they stood outside wondering how to attack the situation, that is, how to get into the party, they were afraid they would be thrown right out. The fear was primarily based on two apparent ex-convicts in suits, parked at the entrance. August had tried going up there, telling them his name: the man had glanced down at some list he was holding for a moment, then he shook his head.

The guys were reproaching August for having dragged them all there, only for them to need to go right back home. As the dissatisfaction neared climax, a woman in a black dress stepped out.

'You look cold; come inside.'

All the boys followed in a line behind the spectacularly beautiful woman. Her hips swayed slightly from side to side as she lured them into the foyer and deeper into the castle. The lights were slightly dimmed, and the music was seductive. The halls were filled with beautiful people dancing and mingling. Cornelia took them throughout the ground floor of the castle and finally ended up in a ballroom with at an oval bar counter attended by several bartenders in black attire.

'Here's a few of my friends, they should be able to entertain your entourage, while I show you something upstairs. Help yourselves to anything you'd like. I'll only borrow your friend for a moment if you don't mind.' She waved him onwards and he left his friends behind, where gleeful smiles were spread all around.

She took him up a grand spiral staircase, holding her small hand behind which August held gently onto. She moved like a cat and he was nervous. She had a strange quality to her, almost as if she was touched by the divine. Whether she really was, or simply believed so herself, didn't matter much. They climbed two stories up when she went down a wide hallway where the walls were stacked up by old stones. She let go of his hand and walked a few paces before him. She held her hand out to the right, with two fingers lightly touching the rugged stone as she moved forward. They continued down the hallway slowly for half a minute when her hand slipped off the stone wall and onto a door handle. She turned her head and smiled coyly.

The room was dark and only lit up by a few candles, which indicated dark walls filled with realistic art, a small round table, and a canopy bed of mahogany wood. On the circular table sat a wide, golden goblet, adorned with Roman gods, filled with ice and a bottle of champagne. She moved over to the table, touching it gently as she circled it while dancing playfully.

'Will you help me open this?' she said.

'With pleasure,' he replied and moved toward her. He opened the bottle and poured two glasses. Her hand brushed against his as he passed her the glass and August had never been more aroused in his life. The whole ordeal was more dreamlike than any dream he could hope to have.

'Thank you for inviting me and my friends,' he tried, not knowing how to proceed.

'The pleasure is all mine.'

'All of this seems a little surreal.'

'Life imitates art far more than art imitates life.'

'What?'

'Do you know who said that?'

'I don't even know what it means, much less who said it.'

'No matter, it's my favorite quote. Do you have one?'

'A favorite quote?'

'Yes.'

August felt embarrassed and confused about her questions. She was clearly embroiled in a world he was unfamiliar with. She appeared cultured, or at least pretended to be, and he wanted badly to impress her. He racked his brain for a clever answer, but the only thing that came to mind was song lyrics by Kanye West. At a loss for words and not wanting to take an abnormally long time to answer the question, he blurted out, 'What doesn't kill you makes you stronger.'

She was surprised by his answer and August's being was filled with shame. He nearly turned around himself and walked out of the room, unwilling to give her the chance to throw him out. But then her surprised face turned into a curious smile, and she said, 'Very good, I also love Nietzsche's works.'

The two of them indulged further in the sparkling delight as their lust grew forcefully. The comment that August felt the scene was surreal, much like a dream, enticed the girl's seduction even more. He had the sense that she was playing some role, being something she wasn't, but he didn't care. This was the person she wanted him to see, and that was enough. Her confidence was both refreshing and novel, as he had never met anyone that direct and playful. He was powerless before her, and it felt exhilarating.

They were sitting on the bed with glasses in hand when she suddenly stood up. She handed him her glass and lightly placed two fingers underneath each of the shoulder straps of her dress.

'Drink up,' she murmured before pushing her fingers outward, causing the black dress to fall to the floor, revealing her bare figure. She had been blessed with the figure of Aphrodite and the curves of her body resembled marble more than human flesh.

With weak legs, August staggered down the spiral staircase an hour later. As he descended, his friends were enjoying the company of beautiful girls on the dance floor. August went over to the bar and fetched a draft beer. He then collapsed on a nearby leather sofa, thinking, *what did I do to deserve this,* accompanied by a euphoric smile.

20

The local newspaper called August a little over a month after he had been released from prison. They were looking to write a memorial for Mathias and wondered whether he would want to contribute. August didn't want to at all, feeling deeply disgusted by the thought of it, but he couldn't bring himself to say no. He wrote a five-hundred-word piece, recounting what a beautiful person Mathias had been.

Each word of that tiny article caused immense pain. It forced him into thinking about all the good attributes he had had, which were great in number. Mathias hadn't been a horrible person at all. Although he had done a horrendous thing or two, generally, he was a loving and agreeable person. And if one is honest, who doesn't do a few reprehensible things here and there?

In the article, he recounted vacations they had shared, wonderful memories at primary school, and Mathias' impressive athletic prowess. The last sentence was: 'A great loss to a wonderful family, but a greater loss for our community and nation who sorely needs strong-spirited men like Mathias.'

It was a vile undertaking, and he cursed himself for accepting the task. Worst of all, it was received tremendously and widely, and he got uplifting comments from all arenas of life. All that positivity didn't matter. That wretched undertaking had broken something in August, something he was hard-pressed to rectify. The walls of justifications he had successfully built came tumbling down as he reflected on all of Mathias' favorable qualities, for that damn tribute. So, what if he had done a few reprehensible things? Nothing justified him being placed six feet underground. And at such a young age, with his whole life ahead of him.

'It's me that shoved him into the abyss,' he thought, reflecting on a dream he had the other night; two people were standing on small floating plateaus made of rock, and below them was a deep abyss. August had to choose who would be put to death and before him stood Mathias and his cousin, Harald, whom he hadn't seen for months. 'He's blood; I can't very well kill him,' he had concluded, sending Mathias off into the darkness.

At first, he found the positive attention pleasant, but after the publication of the memorial, dread increasingly occupied August's being. All the wonderful interactions were tainted by the dye of the lie he was living. If they had any idea, I would be stoned, he thought once, sitting at a table among friends during lunch. These feelings kept mounting over time; eventually, he only managed to get through the days with the constant reminder that in half a year he would be able to travel somewhere far away. He would go study somewhere nobody knew who he was. There he could start over. There he could reinvent himself and attempt to justify his wretched existence.

During the weekends he plunged deeper and deeper into hedonistic pleasure—drinking too much, meaningless sex, and daring activities. All were an effort to dull the pain that was his life.

How could everything have changed so quickly? Before the article, he was on top of the world. He felt that nothing could tear him down. In reality, it took little—a simple reminder of what he had done did the trick. Tom's advice about owning up to your conscience was a thought that August often revisited. That damn criminal was right; although he had tricked himself momentarily, an underground reservoir of guilt never left him. After the release from prison, there was a part of him that whispered in the quiet hours of the day: *this hubris will pass; you know what you've done*. The solution had been to fill the days with excitement and leave as little room for silence as possible. It didn't work out in the end, as that voice made its presence increasingly known.

Thankfully, he found a little solace in alcohol, which he started consuming regularly. He stayed sober Monday and Tuesday, but the rest of the week he would find moments to drink. His friends were only too keen on indulging, which meant the cost burden was also shared. Drinking is expensive in Norway, so having friends and admirers who supported his habits was essential. He found that the alcohol reignited a small part of the near manic positive state he had experienced for a small while. It was an important part of why he kept returning to the alcohol. It also helped alleviate some pain, and he found that talking to women became easier.

He remembered a conversation he had with Rickard once, talking about alcohol. The old man was an alcoholic, which was something August never wanted to become. He frankly found it a little repulsive and asked him why he drank so often, as he knew how bad it was. Rickard didn't seem to believe in good and bad, so it didn't concern him much. He was interested in the felt experience of life and found that alcohol contributed to that in some manner. At the same time, he wasn't ignorant of the unhealthy nature of the poison. August had also weighed the pros and cons of drinking, and at this point in his life he found himself aligned with the homeless man.

21

A part of August rejoiced in his friend's killing. How dared he go behind his back and steal his first love? Who does something like that other than some slimy, devilish creature? It's one of those things you only read in novels or find in cheesy movies, but it had happened to him. *Why me?* He had often wondered. God, what an embarrassment that whole ordeal had been. Nothing could have made it okay, but maybe it would have helped some if Mathias had been upfront about what had happened. If he had asked August how he felt about it? If it was all right with him, which it wouldn't have been, but he would have said yes anyhow. No, that wasn't what happened at all. August had to discover for himself that they were sneaking around. Well, probably everyone knew except him, but that's how those things go.

It was a conflicting feeling, two parts of himself bashing up against each other. One being righteousness and the other his conscience. He couldn't very well tell himself that killing him was the right thing to do, but it didn't feel unwarranted either. These were some thoughts that plagued August as he mulled over his recent history every night before bed.

'I had the strangest dream last night,' said August when he arrived at the dining table for breakfast.

August had a habit of telling his mother about his dreams, as she had always encouraged her children to tell her in the morning whenever they remembered them. They are awfully interesting and informative, she had assured them. And she also said that nature didn't waste energy, so only fools ignore their dreams. She had a fair point.

'Oh, do tell!'

'I was living on a large plot of land, a farm of a kind, where we had cattle, sheep, and horses wandering around. I sat out on the porch in an old rocking chair with a drink in my hand. I think it was whiskey? And from inside the house, I heard screams. Horrible screams. It was my wife in labor with our third child. I thought about whether I should go in to support her somehow but decided against it. Instead, I simply sat there as the sun dawned, sipping my cocktail with a tremendous feeling of uneasiness.'

'Very interesting. How did you feel when you woke up?'

'I don't know exactly. Maybe a little distraught.'

'Well, no wonder, leaving your wife to fend for herself like that! Haha, yeah, very, very interesting. Did you recognize the place, or did it remind you of anywhere?'

'Not really.'

'And you said the sun was setting?'

'Yes, that's right. Oh, and there was something else too.'

'What!?'

'There was an eagle, or perhaps a vulture, that kept circling our house up above. Yes, I remember it was a large part of that uneasiness I felt.'

'Well, that sounds like an ominous sign.'

'Tell me about it.'

'Well, you sit with those images, and maybe something helpful will pop up. Thank you for telling me, darling.'

The images of the dream stayed with him the whole day, unable to shake them even if he wanted to. The screams from his wife kept ringing in his mind. It had been an agonizing cry of despair and betrayal. He thought about the betrayal he had felt because of Mathias's actions. They paled in comparison to his own doing. There really is no greater betrayal than taking a friend's life. Taking another man's woman and killing their friendship is emotionally destructive. But all things considered, trespassing the cardinal sin of murder is more untenable. These were the thoughts held by August's rational brain, yet his primal being was less convinced.

That day was spent walking endlessly around the city and the forests of Drøbak. A restless feeling had taken refuge in August's body and wouldn't let go. This tension of a bad deed containing something good or righteous was troubling the young man. Wandering through the small town, a heavy grief weighed him down. Almost as if this would be the last time he would see the city. A part of him was bidding it all farewell, and it hurt. He didn't want to say goodbye to this place, the peaceful and lovely little village he had grown up in. He had run along these gravel sidewalks all his life and knew most everyone he ran into. There was another aspect of the grief, namely the isolation that came with all the judgement related to Mathias's death. For a long time, he had felt alone. An outcast, banished from society, practically speaking. Now, by some miracle, he had been let back into the warmth of belonging, but not long ago he stood out in the cold, looking in through the misty window of the cozy cabin that is social life. This experience tinged his world view. It all felt so artificial now, as if built on sand, ready to break down at any moment's notice, threatening to cast him back into the abyss of instability.

The whistle of the wind sang a depressing tune as he made his way through the park. Wide trunks and slim branches reached far into the sky and overhung his lowered head. An unsettling dizziness crept into August as he neared the cliff; they had discarded his best friend. He began feeling nauseated and started searching for the closest bench. An older woman was already sitting at the first bench he found, so under normal circumstances he would find another. But not this time, as his body didn't leave him a choice.

'Do you mind if I sit?'

'Not at all, please sit down,' she replied with a smile, and sensing his discomfort, she continued, 'Is everything okay?'

'Yeah, I am alright. I just feel a little nauseous.'

'I have some water in my bag, would you like some?' she asked without waiting for an answer, producing a bottle of water before him.

'Thank you.'

People walked by, and clouds danced across the sky above them while they sat in silence. August was gathering himself and felt grateful to the older woman.

'How are you doing?' he eventually said.

'I am a little down to tell you the truth. I lost a friend recently, a kind-hearted man, or so I thought. Anyway, it's been bothering me quite a lot.'

'I'm sorry.'

'Thank you, no, it's okay, really. The sun is shining, and I am still here, aren't I? What is there to complain about.'

August nodded politely, unsure how to respond to morbid humor in older folk.

'And how are you, young man? I know who you are, of course. Well, everyone does. It must be a pain, everyone knowing you, no? Meanwhile, you've got little clue who we are.'

She was right: it felt overwhelming with all the glances and people talking of you with covered mouths.

'I am okay. It is a little strange, but I don't mind it much. I guess it's a little cool that people know me.'

'Yet, no one really knows that, do they? Know who you are.'

The comments made him flush, and he felt like he was back in the police interviews.

'What do you mean?'

'Well, isn't that what all the celebrities say? People just know their faces and names, believing that they also know who they really are, but in actuality people have no clue. I think that would drive me up a wall. I'm probably talking too much; forgive me.'

His shoulders lowered as he understood she wasn't passing suspicion. He smiled and reassured her it was no problem at all.

'Rickard mentioned you once or twice.' she said suddenly.

The ease that had built up in August was eroded in a moment. The nausea that had come under his control and settled was now returning with a vengeance.

'I am so sorry you had to go through all that senseless hardship. As if losing a good friend wasn't enou—' But before the lady could finish her sentence, August threw his ailing body across the handle of the park bench and emptied his bowels.

The old woman jumped up in a fright, unsure of what to do, but her maternal instincts brought her over to the boy, petting his back gently.

'So, so, it's alright. When something wants to come out, it's best to let it. Here, have some more water,' she said, after he finished and had caught his breath. With bloodshot eyes he forced a large gulp of water down his acidic throat.

22

The annual winter gala for graduating high school students fell on the second Friday of December. August and his friends had been looking forward to it for years now. It was scheduled a little earlier than usual, but that happened to be the only date the school could rent the magnificent locale of Oscarsborg. It was a small fortification placed on an island in the Oslofjord, right outside of Drøbak. These days it also served as a museum and was a frequent destination for tourists and boat owners. It was ordained with old cannons placed around the little island, as it had functioned as a stronghold during WWII. On the island, there was a small castle built in stone that housed a somewhat grand ballroom beneath a tall ceiling.

To get to Oscarsborg, one needed to take a boat, either one's own or the commercial ferry that left from a few spots of Drøbak every two hours from 09:00 till 18:00. At the gala dinner, a three-course menu was served, and a bar was also available for students to buy refreshments, but most of the kids brought their alcohol in plastic bags, hiding it somewhere close to the entrance of the worn-down fort. This resulted in frequent trips for fresh air, where many inebriants were consumed, whether it be drinking or smoking. It was also customary to take a date to the gala, and August had been asked by a beautiful and confident girl named Elisabeth. He happily obliged and looked forward to another night of depravity.

All students were to meet at the last dock visited by the ferry before it carried the passengers over to the little island. The time set for the meet was 17:30. Before heading there, August and his friends gathered at a house lying nearby for predrinks. They played drinking games and had a merry time. All of them showed up at the docks in good spirits. August quickly spotted Elisabeth in an elegant and tight red dress, standing among a group of girls chatting. He made his way over, greeting her by sliding his hand around her waist, to which she smiled and pulled him close.

'You look stunning,' he said, before kissing her on the cheek.

She blushed and thanked him, retorting that he didn't look bad either. They parted ways after a few words and agreed to meet back up at the gala. Before returning to his group of friends, August noticed that Josephine was also a part of the little group. He smiled gently at her, and surprisingly, she smiled back. Instantly, August's being was flooded with ecstasy. He walked back to his friends, engaging in mindless chatter and banter, but his mind did not leave the thought of her alone; her image and the corresponding longing after it did not stop bothering August the whole evening.

The meal was lovely; they were served roasted deer with sides and a glass of red wine. This was included in the ticket and the remaining consumables came out of their own pockets. August sat next to Elisabeth, and they were surrounded by friends on all sides. Their hands switched between each other's thighs throughout the dinner, and August felt intoxicatingly aroused.

Shortly after the dinner finished, the tables were cleared away, making room for the dance floor. Most of the attending teenagers danced, laughed, and enjoyed themselves greatly, with some of the shyer ones staying more to the side, not daring to enter the floor.

The minds of these kids were focused on dance, alcohol, and sex. August, however, was only thinking of one thing—or, one girl, rather. Despite dancing merrily up close to his date, his eyes were turned across the dance floor. There she stood with two girlfriends. Her curly hair rippled mesmerizingly through the air as her body moved pleasingly to the music. A big smile lit up her beautiful face, bringing joy to August's heart. He hadn't seen her smile like that since before Mathias' disappearance.

He eventually made his way toward her, feeling tall on booze. He moved next to her and told her she looked stunning. As the hollow words left his lips, he remembered he had said the same thing to Elisabeth by the docks earlier and cursed his idiocy; hopefully, she hadn't heard me. But she smiled at the comment and showed her gratitude by gently rubbing up against him. They danced for a while, and August felt elated. Then her supple hand grabbed his, and she led him out of the hall. They moved further away from the others, and the music was only a subtle noise in the background now. Coldness lingered in the air of the narrow castle aisle, which they passed through silently. Then she stopped, not knowing where they were nor where to go. August looked into her green eyes revealing a duality of lust and apprehension.

'I just had to get out of there for a minute.'

‘Of course,’ he replied, he grabbed her hand once more and began moving further away from the party.

‘How are you doing?’ August asked.

She thought for a moment, then said, ‘I don’t know exactly.’

They remained quiet, walking slowly until a wooden door appeared on their right. August tryingly led her through the door and she happily complied. It was a small shed with shelves stacked on top of each other on each side, fitted with paper towels and washing equipment. Josephine closed the door behind them and pulled August in, kissing him with her back up against the closed door. It felt as if his feet came off the ground, and lust filled the young man. However, he pulled back after a few seconds, shaking his head and desperately holding back tears that wanted to well forth.

‘This isn’t right,’ he said in despair.

‘What’s wrong?’ Josephine asked, drawing nearer to him.

He reluctantly held his hand out. ‘You don’t want this.’

‘I do want this. I want you.’

This only caused further distress in August, who was struggling to keep a sound mind.

'You don't understand. You don't know me. Not at all.'

He was right about one thing, as she clearly didn't understand what was happening. She looked at him inquisitively.

'What the hell do you mean I don't know you? You're talking complete nonsense. You're drunk!'

A tremendous terror built up in August, who felt both compelled and reluctant to tell her everything. Some strange will inside of him wouldn't let him leave that room till he had said what needed to be said. He fought himself with all his power, but before managing to make the reasonable decision to get out of there, the following spilled forth.

'You cannot tell a soul this, okay?'

He paused until he saw her timid nodding, then he hesitantly continued:

'I'm the reason Mathias is dead. I didn't mean for any of it to happen. I truly didn't. We'd been drinking, and I was upset with how he'd treated you! You don't deserve a man like that! He got on my nerves, and I punched him. I cou… I didn't know what would happen. My whole life feels fucked now: my mind is all scrambled, and all the pain I've caused is killing me. To make matters worse, there's an innocent man in prison because of my actions right now.'

Josephine had difficulties processing what he said, and the disbelief was painted across her face.

'What do you mean, *the way he treated me*?' she stuttered.

'Isn't that obvious?! He abused you, for god's sake,' he screamed.

'Oh god. No, he didn't. What have I done?' she murmured quietly. All at once, the horrid feeling of being trapped in the room with a murderer took hold of her.

'I won't tell a soul. I promise.'

She reassured him with all her will, and when she sensed that his guard had lowered a little, she moved closer to August. She began kissing his neck softly. At first, he felt disgusted; what kind of person is she? Then he was startled, partly because of his stupid admission, but also due to her unsettling eyes. Despite these apprehensions, a huge burden began sliding off his shoulders as she continued kissing him. He didn't stop her and let himself go entirely. Soon they were passionately enveloped in each other's beings. Holding her—and the intoxicating passion of her touch—nearly drove him mad. A blissful exuberance reverberated throughout August as he explored the body of the woman he had once lost and never thought he would possess again.

As the young man walked toward his home that night, he fantasized about the life they would build together. He couldn't think of a time he had been happier, and he was looking forward to what lay ahead.

A few days later, the police showed up at his door and it became clear that he would be arrested once again. This time due to new incriminating testimony. Naturally, August understood he had been betrayed. He felt beaten down and stepped on by the woman he loved all over again. Yet, most of all, he cursed himself for his idiotic behavior. His life, as he knew it, was over now. He had no one to blame but his weak self. But what did it matter? It hadn't been much of a life to speak of lately. It was only a series of disappointments, betrayals, and horrid actions.

August felt a mixture of relief and despair as he decided to face the consequences of his actions. There was no point in hiding or denying it anymore—it was time to be truthful for once—to attempt moving toward becoming a person he would be okay to live alongside. He also started considering the night he had shared with Josephine, which gave rise to tremendous shame. She had only thrown herself at him as a last resort. Anything to get out of the situation alive and well. Yes, it was one big tragic circus, the whole thing, he thought, as he was placed back into a cell, where he would spend the next decades of his sorrowful life. The only solace he clung to was remembering the face of the compassionate old man who had helped him when he was all alone and the comforting thought that he could finally walk freely once more.

23

Initially, there was a strange serenity that accompanied knowing with certitude what the next several years will look like. There would be no leaving the walls and perimeter of the prison, and all the strands of things that can happen in the prison are peculiarly finite. There is a comforting security in knowing what the future holds. He wondered how he would fill the time; he felt unsure but figured he would spend the next few weeks and months sketching out the things he would like to do. He might learn a language or two—Italian had always appealed to him, but he had only learned Spanish in school. There was a workshop at the prison, where one could paint or work with wood, creating furniture and such. He would also have to pick up some card games, as that was the main social activity, outside sitting together before the TV, if one can venture to call that social.

There was also a deadly sterility to this type of life. The optimist will call life an adventure and could put forth a reasonable argument for it. That is, for the life outside these walls. Any optimist will turn sour when locked up. Here, the novelty of life had been turned down to an unfathomably low degree. It is not null, but it feels awfully close. He also worried his parents would abandon him. He couldn't blame them, really. Who would want to keep contact with a monster of a son? He feared they would slowly dwindle their contact with him, stopping altogether after a few months or so. Then he would truly be alone in this world. It was a terrifying thought, and a likely one, in August's mind. He also didn't want them to blame themselves for his actions. It was an accident after all, so there was no blame to hand out, other than his own stupidity. But how could they be sure of that? They can only take their murderous son's word for it.

What an unforgiving and disastrous life this is, he thought as he lay on his hard bed, not able to sleep. He turned the bedside lamp back on and grabbed a small notepad from the table beside him.

There's a deep sadness in my heart as I write this. Dear God, what is the purpose of these dark nights? Why am I punished and misunderstood? Is there a light you are leading toward? Will I ever arrive? I am afraid I don't possess the strength you think I do. If I can't take this life, then what? I really wonder what there is left for me but pity, plight, and sorrow. My whole life—what is it all for? What am I supposed to live for now? Will my remaining days be spent repenting for what I have done? Even if it were so, the positive impact I can make is terribly minuscule here.

I had dreams, you know. I wanted to be a lawyer, or maybe an actor. Yes, a celebrated actor is what I would be, and I would mingle with interesting and beautiful people. I would take part in movies that spoke to people. Deep movies that touched the heart and soul of the viewers, something that prompted a transformation of character even. I want people to fall in love with the life they're given, despite the horridness. The fire that kept those dreams alive has perished now. All that is left are the ashes of long-lost ideas and hopes. What I feared would be difficult has turned impossible.

The pen seems to be living a life of his own as I lie here. There is a deeper sadness embracing me now, than when I started writing this. Moments ago, I didn't even know I wanted to act. I still don't know what to do, but it doesn't matter now, does it? Oh, I hate myself and this terrible, terrible life.

I wonder if one only gets to know what one really wants to do when it's too late? Maybe a few lucky ones catch their inspiration before that time. I sure hope so, but maybe there is something I can do here to prepare myself for the life that follows my sentence. I imagine it will be difficult to find any job after serving several years, but it's not impossible, necessarily. Yes, there may be some strength and vitality to be gathered from working toward this life.

His hand grew tired, and he let the pen fall from his hand. He chucked the notepad to the side and turned over on his side, tucking the blanket between his legs. A rush of pleasant waves circulated his body, and he felt a hint of joy for the first time in weeks. He was shocked at the words that flowed out of him, as if they came from someplace other than himself. He felt he had written something beautiful. Yes, beautiful. And true. He had never had that sensation before, which was strange. That only now, at this point in his life, which for all practical purposes felt like the end, something like that would occur. Almost like a new beginning, a new outlook. He had never sat down before to intentionally write something beautiful. That might also be impossible. Maybe something like that can only arrive in a moment of crisis. Only when one is trapped and hopeless do parts of oneself reveal a sliver of optimism, a new path that you couldn't possibly have found on your own. A path that has the potential of making the future tolerable.

With his eyes half closed, he pondered his dream of becoming an actor. Where did that come from? As a child, he remembered thinking it would be an amazing profession. But why? The attention and glory seemed rather attractive, but there was more to it. To take part in something bigger than yourself, something that affected people. Whether it was making someone laugh, cry, or even turn their lives around—that felt especially exciting to August. He had had a taste of fame too now, which felt thrilling, but that thrill would surely fade away with time. It would even begin to taste sour if one does well enough. So, it must be something else that sustains and revitalizes any proper actor. A few names ran through his head of actors that he knew had a criminal past. Guys like Robert Downey Jr. and Mark Wahlberg were prime examples that a past behind bars didn't destroy your chances. Then again, they weren't convicted of murder.

The next morning, he arose feeling exhausted in his little single unit cell. It was a rather neat place, all considered, and he felt grateful to be Norwegian, as he had seen some show on how prisons looked in the United States. They looked more like rat cages than anything else. In poorer nations the conditions were surely even worse. His cell looked like a four-star hotel room in comparison, so everything truly is relative. With a strange mix of gratitude and sleep deprivation, he rinsed his face with cold water in the hopes of waking himself up.

In the common area, three men were sitting playing cards. Another middle-aged man, Adrian, had moved a chair before the window and was enjoying the view of the calm sky. It was torture, sitting there and looking up, thought August. The window watcher noticed him and waved him over. August grabbed a chair and sat next to him.

'How was your sleep?' Adrian asked enthusiastically.

'Another bad night.'

'It'll get better eventually, trust me. Any plans for today?'

'Oh yes, plenty. It will be a great day.' August retorted with an ironic smile. Both shared a somber laugh, then turned their gaze to the floating clouds above.

'I'll bring you along to the workshop today if you want. I'm working on a rocking chair.'

'Sure,' he replied dryly, before asking what he was making the chair for.

'What do you mean?' said the inmate.

'I mean, why are you wasting a ton of hours creating some silly chair, only for it to be taken away and sold for a profit you'll never see the light of?'

'Well, it's rather easy. Try to think of the alternative, genius.'

'Seems more relaxing to me?'

'To relax is what you want to do? To do nothing at all. Are you sure about that?

'I don't see why not.'

'I understand. That's just your age talking. In fact, it's your immaturity screaming at the top of its lungs! There will be plenty of time to do nothing here, but soon enough you'll find that to be a pretty hollow pursuit.'

'Jesus, relax man. I'll come along to the workshop later, just give me a break.'

The seasoned inmate didn't move his head and was still staring out the window. He gave off a slight smile and a sigh.

That same evening, August put up a note on his bathroom mirror in his cell which read: I will become a renowned actor and movie star. Every morning and every night he stared at that note while brushing his teeth. As he repeated the sentence out loud he felt a burning desire in the pit of his stomach. This fire grew stronger and felt more real as time went on. That was, for a while at least. Five months down the line, the mirror was clean once more. No proud note with affirming words was anywhere in sight. All that remained was a crumbled piece of paper, furnishing the corner of his grubby bathroom.

24

When Rickard received the news that he would be free to go, he felt like an antelope suddenly released from the jaws of a lion: hurt, alone, and unsure where to turn. He grieved August's future and delved into a deep melancholy.

When he finally made it onto the streets, the bitter coldness gripped his being, giving the old man a surge of energy to find refuge to stay alive. It was late December when he was released, and his lousy blazer didn't help much in keeping the warmth. He did discover a pleasant surprise, however, as a dirty fifty note had been hidden in the inner pocket of his jacket. He wondered whether he had had the ingenious idea of putting it there just in case of unforeseen events but concluded it was more likely dumb luck. With some wealth to his name, he made his way to the central station of Oslo. He found the bus heading to Drøbak, stepped on, and used the last money to his name to buy a ticket.

As he slumped down on the seat, a little warmth slowly gathered in his being again. It felt pleasant, and he wanted to stay on the bus indefinitely. Thankfully, there was one thing that produced a sliver of joy in the otherwise despondent old man: the thought of seeing Martha again. By now she had heard that August had been arrested again, meaning he would probably be welcome to stay at her warm and jovial place. She had never sent him a letter nor called him in jail, but that was understandable, he thought, as she had probably thought that he was a guilty man.

He stepped off the bus onto the city square of Drøbak. Snow was falling gently from above, and the streets were deserted. Rickard pulled his blazer tightly around his frail body, trying to kill the small gaps that opened the door to the cold air. It didn't help as it was horridly chilly. The type of coldness one cannot hope to fight off without appropriate clothing, clothing that he did not possess. Snow and ice covered the ground, with another ten centimeters of fresh snow resting on top. He shuffled his feet through the snow, which began filling his shoes. It only took a minute before the snow that had snuck into his shoe had melted, turning them into cold lakes. He prayed to God that he'd give him warmth as he made his way up Damveien. He dragged his suitcase along with him, but it was heavy and he was getting winded.

He alternated between carrying it and sliding it in the snow. It was late evening, and the dark sky above was littered with sublime stars. The people of Drøbak had settled and enjoyed the evening in the warmth of family and a heated house. Rickard glanced into several windows on the way. One family of five sat around the dining table, having a merry time. Another family had gathered before the TV, watching some entertainment show and laughing so loud it escaped their wooden walls.

In the house right before Martha's, he spotted two children sitting before an old fireplace with a lively flame. They sat next to each other, playing with little wooden sticks, creating their miniature campfires. The powerful sensation of déjà vu came over Rickard, who was reminded of sitting before a fireplace with his own child. A sadness spread across his face, and a tear shimmered in the corner of his eye. He stood there looking at these innocent angels for a while, forgetting all about where he was going and the biting cold. Then he looked up at the night sky, imagining her sitting up there somewhere looking down. What a pitiful sight she must have seen; he was old and cold with no place to call home. Staying behind as she took flight had changed his life, and his road thereafter had been littered with pain and difficulties. But he had found a path. Step by step, he had made his way forward, although many times he considered taking an early exit.

One must not take pity on the dead but on the people that remain. Death is a cruel mistress that deals in absolutes; she provides and takes, grants and steals. She's a wicked partner we all travel alongside, and few were more familiar with her gait than Rickard. One day we'll all step into oblivion and find out what waits behind the veil. Those of us who have felt the lingering and soft touch of death may have intimations of what comes. It sure must be sweeter than this life is, he thought.

He continued walking a few paces and landed before Martha's gateway. He opened the gate and fixed his gaze on the house; it was dark. He thought it strange as he scanned the windows. Maybe she had gone to sleep? It wouldn't be too shocking considering her age. Standing there, before the opened gate, just about to head in, he heard soft footsteps approaching. He turned around and saw a middle-aged man with dark features coming closer. He wore a black overcoat and looked curiously at the old freezing man.

'Hi there, are you looking for Martha?'

Rickard felt he recognized him, but he couldn't exactly place him.

'I am, yes. Do you know if she's out?'

The man appeared taken aback and his eyebrows rose on his otherwise apathetic face.

'Why, you mustn't have heard. She passed away two weeks back. Were you friends?'

Rickard didn't expect to hear those words, and grief's wicked hands took hold of him. His legs began feeling unsteady. He took a few steps to the side, then slid down onto the cold and wet ground, with his back leaning against Martha's fence. His hands came up and rubbed his eyes ferociously; utter chaos began wreaking havoc inside of him, as the last frivolous piece he thought remained was pushed off the board completely.

'I'm sorry for your loss,' the man continued with a thin smile, bordering on devious.

Rickard sat there with his head planted in his cold hands as he heard the man's footsteps move further and further away. Inertia enveloped the tired man, who didn't know where to turn or what to do. There was no longer energy to do anything. All he could manage was to sit still. To sit there, in the abrasive cold, reflecting on

August's tragic fate, whom he could not rescue and to give another chance at life, and Martha's kind spirit he would never have the joy of accompanying once more.

A bitterness foamed and salivated in his mouth. The damn wickedness of life wouldn't take leave of him for a moment. One bitter event after the other. It was comical really—and had it not been his own life, he would have laughed.

Then a surge of energy, given by the faithful mistress of all, brought him to his feet. He wobbled down towards the harbor, as a strange urge to possess and be enveloped by the sea was overpowering. The stars danced above him, singing transfixing tunes, as he moved toward the primeval mother. He made it to the glimmering water, lit up by the moon, and leaned up against a statue. It was a statue he had passed thousands of times before, and his gaze rose to her face. She looked sternly ahead as if showing the way. His eyes followed the rest of her body and traced it to the tip of her hand, pointing out toward the ocean. A warmth spread through his chest, and his gaze returned to the water. A magnificent voice could be heard from out there, beckoning him on:

'You've done your part. It's time to let go; this way, here in my soft arms. Come, lay your tired head in my lap. Come now, my dear child.'

You're tired and cold
Take my gait and sing along
My bellowing voice will
Rejoice as you fold
Back into the water cold
You've seen me before
You'll see me again
My child this is life
Little and large
Sins and farces
Come now, come now
All you've been told
Nothing but memories old

www.ingramcontent.com/pod-product-compliance
Lightning Source LLC
La Vergne TN
LVHW091143080826
845145LV00008B/2237